Petal Plucker

Funny, charming, and utterly captivating! I devoured this sparkling read.

— ANNIKA MARTIN, NEW YORK TIMES BESTSELLING AUTHOR

Petal Plucker was funny, entertaining, fresh and fan-yourself-worthy . . . Their enemies-to-lovers romance is both charming, tender and steamy, and you'll love both of these characters (and their families!) and their sigh-worthy happily ever after.

— MARY DUBÉ, CONTEMPORARILY EVER AFTER

Morland has created a masterpiece of a romance . . . one of my favorite [books] of the year.

— CRISTIINA READS

Humorous, raunchy, and refreshing, Petal Plucker has rightfully earned its way, in my opinion, as one of the best romantic comedy [books] this year.

— CAROL, TIL THE LAST PAGE

My One and Only

This book was gripping, well written & the chemistry between the characters sizzled throughout this wonderful read.

— AMAZON REVIEW

All I Want Is You

Another heartfelt, steamy, terrific story. This is an author who really knows how to create a story that catches a reader's attention and characters that capture her heart.

— BOOKADDICT

Taking a Chance on Love

Thea and Anthony are in for a surprise when it comes to the language of the heart . . . I am in awe.

— HOPELESS ROMANTIC BLOG

Then Came You

This story really pulled all my heartstrings. This was truly a beautiful story and makes you believe there really is true love out there.

— MEME CHANELL BOOK CORNER

ALSO BY IRIS MORLAND

ROMANTIC COMEDIES

He Loves Me, He Loves Me Not

Petal Plucker

War of the roses

LOVE EVERLASTING

including

THE YOUNGERS

Then Came You

Taking a Chance on Love

All I Want Is You

My One and Only

THE THORNTONS

The Nearness of You

The Very Thought of You

If I Can't Have You

Dream a Little Dream of Me

Someone to Watch Over Me

Till There Was You

I'll Be Home for Christmas

Heron's Landing

Seduce Me Sweetly

Tempt Me Tenderly

Desire Me Dearly

Adore Me Ardently

HE LOVES ME, HE LOVES ME NOT

THE FLOWER SHOP SISTERS

IRIS MORLAND

For everyone who gave this quirky little series a chance.

HE LOVES ME, HE LOVES ME NOT

CHAPTER ONE

MARI

The moment I woke up after my best friend's raucous bachelorette party in Las Vegas, I realized two things in quick succession:

1. I was spooning with a man who was very, very naked.
2. And I had no idea who he was.

To my horror, the man had his arm slung across me, and it weighed at least a thousand pounds, I was sure. My bladder yelled profanities at me as I pushed at the ridiculously heavy arm trapping me against the bed.

Finally, he turned over, taking his arm with him. I shuffled to the bathroom and didn't feel the panic hit me until after I'd peed and saw the ring on my left hand.

Ring. Left hand. I didn't wear a ring there anymore since I'd caught my ex-fiancé cheating on me. I'd thrown the ring David had bought me in his face.

This ring wasn't that diamond David had gotten me. I

peered more closely at it. It was—plastic? Was it from a *ring pop?*

Did I call the police? No, that was stupid. *911, I got married last night to a stranger.* Yeah, that'd go over well. I was sure the Vegas police would just laugh and tell us to get a lawyer.

I heard movement in the room. I froze. Glancing in the mirror, I saw a wild-eyed woman with bedhead, smeared lipstick, raccoon eyes from melted mascara, and a whole bunch of hickeys across my collarbone.

I very rarely swore, but at that moment I wanted to swear until I was blue in the face.

What had I done last night? And who was in my bed with me?

I wasn't that kind of girl—you know, the wild girl. The girl who had one-night stands in Vegas. The girl who threw caution to the wind.

I'd been about to get married to a man who drove a Prius and was an accountant. I always got the perfect attendance certificate in elementary school. I'd been one of the valedictorians at my high school; I'd gotten an A- *once* because my teacher had dared to think my essay on fashion in *The Great Gatsby* was "insipid, at best." (She'd been wrong, by the way.)

I was Marigold Wright, and I was a good girl.

I prided myself on my good girl-ness. Where my sisters were either oddballs or outright deviants (at least in my mind), I never crossed lines. I liked lines. Lines were comforting. They existed for a reason; otherwise the world would be in utter chaos.

My one real indulgence in life was my makeup obsession. My collection was scattered across the bathroom counter—an excessive amount of products for one person on a brief trip—

and strangely enough, having this man see it all seemed like a violation of my privacy. Even more than being in bed with me and him being naked. I began to put my makeup away, knowing in my haste I'd have to go through it and reorganize it when I got home.

"Are you done in there?" a growling male voice said through the bathroom door. "I'm fuckin' dying out here." An accent tinged his speech, but I was too tired to try to place it.

I tossed the last products into my makeup bag and scrubbed at my face. Realizing it didn't matter, I opened the door with a frigid expression.

The man—who wore only a sheet draped around his hips —smiled down at me. No, he didn't smile; he smirked. I'd never been the recipient of a true smirk before, but this man clearly had perfected the look.

He was tall, so tall I had to tilt my head back. He had to be at least six-five; I was five-ten, so it was rare that men were tall enough that I felt short in comparison. But what arrested me most was how dark his eyes were. Oh, and the fact that he was jacked. Muscles for days, his chest covered in dark hair that matched the beard shadowing his cheeks and jaw.

"Are you done or can I take a piss now?" he said.

I blushed to the roots of my hair. Being a redhead, my blushes tended to be bright and extremely obvious, and this man in front of me seemed very amused with my red cheeks. I wanted to ask him if he remembered what had happened last night, but it was as if the words had dried up in my throat.

Or maybe it was because I had a large male glaring down at me because I wouldn't let him pee.

"Be my guest," I said, ducking under his arm. I tried to

look as prim as I could, but it was difficult when I looked like a total wreck and didn't even know this man's name.

He shut the door with an ironic bow, giving me some time to collect my thoughts. Actually, I didn't need to collect my thoughts: I needed to *run.* But as I got dressed and began to toss things into my suitcase, I realized he was the one who needed to leave. This was *my* room.

I stopped packing when memories started to surface, like images from a movie. I remembered stumbling down the Las Vegas strip, and I could remember this man's voice beside me. Then the bachelorette party where the bride-to-be, Jenna, kept shoving tequila shots in front of me. Or had that happened before we'd stumbled down the strip?

Worst of all, I remembered the touch of a man—this man —who made heat lick through my veins.

But he wasn't just any man. He had a name. I remembered that now, because we'd met the day prior to the bachelorette party.

Liam. His name was Liam, but his last name eluded me at the moment. He'd sat next to me at the rehearsal dinner, and then at the hotel pool after that—

Oh God, had I slept with him last night? Based on the hickeys, it certainly seemed plausible. But I couldn't remember, and that made my stomach curdle.

I needed a bottle of water, ibuprofen, and some explanations. I scrambled around in my suitcase, only to find a gift bag from the bachelorette party the night before. Right as I pulled out a pink dildo that said *Pleasure for* your *pink* on the base, Liam emerged from the bathroom.

"I'm flattered, love, but pink isn't really my color," he said over my shoulder. "Besides the fact that I'm always the one who does the penetrating," he added with a wry chuckle.

I tried to stuff the dildo back into the bag, but I only proceeded to empty the rest of its contents, which included: a handful of condoms—ribbed for her pleasure, so obviously there was a theme here; a butt plug with a diamond handle; and a bullet vibe that started buzzing way too enthusiastically for my pounding head.

I could've cheerfully strangled Jenna for giving us these party favors last night. Whatever happened to a piece of jewelry or a gift certificate from Starbucks? Something benign, something that didn't involve things that went up your butt. Although anything could become a butt plug if you really tried, I reasoned.

"Oh my God," I groaned. "This isn't happening. This isn't happening. This isn't happening—"

I turned to face Liam, only to see that he was naked.

And no, the dildo was no match for him. Jesus Christ on a stick, how could a man look that good naked? He didn't have an ounce of fat on him. He was built like a linebacker, although, admittedly, I didn't know exactly how any football player should look. I'd always been more into slender guys.

Then again, my slender in all things ex-fiancé had cheated on me so my taste in men was clearly suspect.

Liam just waited for me to speak. He wasn't at all embarrassed by his nudity, and based on how perfectly built he was he had no reason to be modest. To my utter shock, he was soon half-hard.

I watched in fascination as his cock grew before my very eyes. He had a delicious V that cut past his hips and pointed straight to his package. I wanted to lick both of those lines until I reached his cock—

I finally found my voice, because I did not have time to stare at a semi-stranger's erection. "Put some clothes on!" I screeched. "And get out of my room!"

He crossed his arms over his broad chest, that dumb smirk on his handsome face. "Last night wasn't that bad."

Last night? I scowled. "I'm not having this discussion until you put some pants on."

"Funny, considering how much you wanted them off last night."

I ignored that remark, even though butterflies exploded inside my stomach. That was probably from the alcohol still digesting, I thought. Or maybe I was still drunk. I touched my forehead, as if being drunk were the same as having a fever and thus diagnosable.

I suddenly felt perilously close to tears, but I knew it would only make my headache worse. I pulled my hair back into a tight ponytail, ignoring Liam behind me getting dressed. My heart pounded so hard that I felt light-headed.

"You can look now. I'm decent," he said.

I turned, noting that, despite the fact that he was dressed, he did not look decent. At all. His collared shirt stretched across his chest, accentuating the width of his shoulders, while he'd rolled the sleeves up his arms to showcase his muscular forearms. He radiated a combination of masculinity and blatant confidence that edged into arrogance.

I didn't know what to do with men like him. David had never radiated anything but safety. Consistency.

Boredom, my mind whispered.

"What happened last night?" I whispered.

Liam lifted a dark eyebrow and sat down on the edge of the still disheveled bed. "You really don't remember?" Once again, his accent made my toes curl into the plush hotel room carpet. He'd told me where he was from—hadn't he?

God, how much tequila had I drunk? I didn't do things like this for a reason. I was the friend who drove drunk friends home.

"I really don't remember," I said in exasperation. "I mean, it's coming back, but…" I was too afraid to ask if we'd slept together.

"You look like you're about to vomit. Is it me or is it the hangover?"

I held up my left hand. "Do you know what this is?"

"Is this a trick question?"

I pointed to the plastic ring. "What. Is. This?"

"A ring, clearly."

He was toying with me, the jerk.

"Why am I wearing it?" I tried again.

"Why the bloody hell would I know that?"

Once again I tried to place his accent—it sounded American at times, but then he'd roll his r's, as if he were savoring the consonants with his tongue.

Based on his exasperation, he didn't know what had happened last night any more than I did.

"Well, I'm wearing a ring on my left hand. That leads me to think…"

Liam turned pale right as the jangled pieces of memories in my brain began to assemble themselves.

Oh God. Oh God, no, no, we couldn't have done *that.*

Memories once again flashed across my eyes. Hands gripping me as I was pressed against a brick wall outside. The sound of slot machines, and Liam yelling when he won a round of blackjack.

White flowers that had been abandoned somewhere between the chapel and the hotel after our wedding ceremony.

Wedding. Ceremony. The ring on my finger. Wedding night.

No, no, no, *no*.

I trembled. I wondered if I was going to swoon at Liam's feet, and I'd never fainted in my entire life.

"Did we—?" My voice croaked. I couldn't say the words, because then it would make them real.

Liam looked like he might faint, too, which would've been funny if not for the circumstances. He then swore in a language I didn't recognize. And then he went to my bag—the one filled with various sex toys—and pulled out a piece of paper. He swore again.

"What? What is that?" I said.

He handed it to me. It was a marriage license, and the two signatures at the bottom?

Marigold Wright and *Liam Gallagher.*

"Oh my God. We're *married?*" The marriage license fluttered to the floor.

"Seems so. Christ." Liam began to pace.

Right then, my foot hit the bag of sex toys, setting off the vibrator. Its buzzing sound filled the room like an alarm. *Danger, danger, you married a man you don't even know!*

I rubbed my temples. Despite the ibuprofen I'd taken, my headache threatened to return in full force after this revelation.

"Can you just tell me what happened last night? After we

got married? Because I can't remember if we slept together or not. That's the one piece that's a blur."

"Now I'm offended," said Liam, stopping to stare at me. "That my brand-new wife can't even remember if she slept with me last night."

"So we didn't have sex?"

Liam snorted. "You'd remember. I'd make sure of it. Women never forget when I've fucked them."

I would've laughed at that outlandish statement, except Liam seemed completely serious. And I had a feeling he wasn't boasting, either.

All of these revelations felt like someone launching a dead, smelly fish at my face. Kind of like the fish they throw at Pike Place Market in Seattle, except the fish were slimy, old, and smelled like garbage and intense regret.

Liam was my fish. He was my stinky, disgusting, rotting fish who also happened to be sinfully handsome and had a huge, delightful cock.

Now my mind was imagining actual fish with actual dicks, and my gorge rose. Penises and fish just did not mix.

Liam's face creased. "You okay?"

I was going to—I didn't know. Puke, cry, laugh. Could you do all three at once? Was there a word for that?

Under the dictionary, there should be a word for what I'd done last night. Synonyms would include: *idiot, moron,* and *imbecile.* Antonyms would include: *Mari Wright up until she got drunk last night and married a stranger.*

Liam glanced at his watch, sighing. "Whatever the fuck happened last night, we can't talk about it now. We need to get going."

At my obvious confusion, he said almost blithely, "Isn't

there a wedding we're supposed to attend? If I do recall, you're the maid of honor."

Now I was really going to vomit. Jenna and Sam's wedding was today. And if I didn't leave this room now, I'd be late to get my hair done for their evening ceremony.

Oh, and now I remembered: Liam was Sam's best man, and I was walking with him down the aisle.

Great, just great.

I pointed a finger in Liam's direction. "Don't say a word about this to anyone. You got that? Because if you do, I'll murder you. After the wedding is over, we'll figure out how to make this right. Okay?"

"You think I wanted this any more than you?" He helped me off the floor, and his touch on my arm was electric. "That I marry random women in Vegas just for fun?"

"I don't know you, so maybe you do it all the time."

His grip was firm, his hands warm, and gazing into his eyes, the spark I'd felt two days ago returned. Liam seemed to sense it, too, because he caressed my cheek with surprisingly gentle fingers. He then touched the hickeys dotting my neck.

"Now I do remember making these," he said ruefully.

I couldn't do this. I pushed his arm away, which was pointless because he was made of either bricks or marble and it did a grand total of nothing.

My stomach lurched right then. I ran to the bathroom, slammed the door closed, and puked my guts up until I was pretty sure I'd vomited up at least one internal organ in the process.

It was just too bad I couldn't puke Liam Gallagher—my *husband*—from my stomach.

CHAPTER TWO

MARI

Two days earlier…

I cocked my head, squinting at the ice sculpture that sat in the middle of the expansive table.

"Is that an ice penis?" I said.

Laura, one of Jenna's bridesmaids, moved more closely to the statue. It was so dim in the private room at the restaurant that neither of us could tell if the statue was actually endowed or not.

"I think so, but it's pretty small. It could also just be its balls," said Laura.

"Why would they sculpt a pair of balls but no penis?"

Laura shrugged. "It's Vegas. Don't ask questions." She flashed a smile. "If it has a dick, it's currently melting off."

"Too bad that can't happen to men in real life," I muttered.

Laura shot me a look, but soon we were overtaken by the rest of the wedding party. Jenna and Sam hadn't skimped one bit on this wedding: each had ten attendants, and apparently there were close to three hundred guests.

Sam's family came from money—something to do with creating the first mechanical litter box—and this was the most extravagant wedding I'd ever attended. The thought that a box that scooped cat poop had financed this Vegas wedding never failed to make me giggle.

Soon we were seated for dinner, the groomsmen and bridesmaids sitting next to each other. I was next to Jenna, who sat at one end of the table; across from me was Sam's college roommate, Mac. Mac was charming and, according to him, "gayer than rainbow sherbet with rainbow sprinkles on top."

To my left was an empty chair—apparently the best man had yet to show up. I'd never met him, but according to Jenna he'd been Sam's best friend since they'd been kids.

It didn't matter, though. I wasn't here to sleep with a groomsman. I mostly wanted to forget that I was supposed to already be married by now. I'd almost thought about telling Jenna I didn't want to come, but she'd asked me to be her maid of honor for a reason. I couldn't flake just because David had broken my heart, stomped on it, and then ground it up in the food processor he'd bought on sale at Kohl's last Christmas.

Mac and Jenna chatted while I popped olives into my mouth, watching water drip from the naked ice sculpture. Currently, the statue's butt was dripping water, as if his cheeks were sweating from the desert heat.

"Is that statue's arse melting?" said a voice over my shoulder.

"Liam! You're here!" Jenna launched from her chair, a

little unsteady already from her wine consumption, and waved to Sam. "Look who finally showed up!"

To my annoyance, Liam wasn't some troll like I'd hoped: he was *handsome.* His features included a sharp jaw, dark hair, and wide shoulders.

I was glad, in a shallow way, that I'd worn my favorite dress—a black number that showed off my legs and shoulders —and had done my sultry, violet makeup look that made my green eyes pop.

Makeup had always been a creative outlet for me since I was a teenager, and I wasn't above using it to my advantage. In this case, I wanted to feel like I was on the same playing field as this godlike, male specimen. Makeup was like a suit of armor: it could cover up my flaws and vulnerability and transform me into a different, stronger person. Or at least a more attractive one.

Once upon a time, I'd wanted to become a makeup artist, but I'd put that dream aside. I preferred practicality over dreams. It was always the safer bet.

"Liam, you'll be right here. Mari, this is Liam. She's the maid of honor," said Sam after he and Liam had hugged.

"Pleasure," Liam drawled as he took my hand. His grip was firm, his hand much bigger than mine. He was so big, yet somehow managed to move with surprising grace as he pulled out his chair and sat next to me.

"I know you probably would've liked to sit by Sam, but we wanted everyone to talk to someone they didn't know," said Jenna in a rush.

Liam slanted me a glance. "It's not a problem."

Not only was he handsome, but his voice was tinged with an accent that I wish didn't make me melt. But I was human, female, and American. God knows we love a good accent.

And now I was supposed to talk to Liam? I was supposed to chat with Mac. Not this man who was clearly not married and not gay, based on the way his gaze raked me. Although I wore a dress that hardly showed any cleavage, he looked at me like I had my breasts out on the table for everyone to see.

I wished I was still engaged. That always made men leave me alone. It was like I'd had a sign on that said *property of another man.* It was archaic and vaguely insulting, yet I wished for that protection right now. I was exposed. I was in a place of limbo in my life. And I was very, very unattached.

You want Liam to see you as attractive, but not too *attractive?* I thought. Yes, I'd admit that sometimes the most confusing person I knew was myself.

But I also couldn't be blatantly rude, so I said, "Do you live in Seattle, too?"

"For the moment," was his bland answer.

"I grew up there. I've never lived anywhere else. It's a great place to raise a family." I was chattering. Blushing, I forced myself to stop talking.

I was grateful when the first course arrived. I could focus on the scallops, not on the man to my left.

Liam's elbow brushed mine as he began to eat, which was the usual hazard when you were left-handed like me. Yet instead of feeling annoyed at the contact, I felt…excited. *Get it together, Mari. Are you seriously getting turned on brushing elbows with a guy?*

"You're left-handed?" said Liam.

"What?"

He looked at me holding my fork. "Switch seats with me."

"Oh, it's fine—"

"Switch." He pulled out my chair, and I could've sworn his fingers brushed my shoulder. On purpose? Or an accident?

"Oh, Mari, I forgot. I'm sorry," said Jenna.

"It's fine." Liam handed me my wineglass, our fingers definitely brushing. His smile was slow and knowing, like he knew how easily he could get a woman to toss her panties in his direction. Like I needed to throw my underwear at any man's head right now.

"So, Mari was it? Tell me about yourself," said Liam.

He rolled the *r* in my name, making it sound more exotic than it was.

I considered the question. "Like I said, I'm from Seattle. I work as a technical writer. That's about it."

"That's it? You don't do anything for fun?"

"I'm too busy to have fun these days."

He looked me up and down. "That's a damn shame, then."

"Thanks." I rolled my eyes. "Do you always insult people you've just met?"

He smiled, his teeth flashing. "Are you always so uptight?"

"Now you're just being rude."

"I prefer to say I'm honest. Besides, I doubt you're telling the truth. I'm sure you do fun things sometimes. You just won't tell me."

"No, I never have fun. Ever. I'm normal and boring and not worth talking to."

He chuckled, the sound dry and raspy. "I doubt that. I've never met a redhead who was any of those things."

I snorted. I'd always resisted the idea that since my hair was red, then I should be feisty and fiery and all number of things that didn't describe me at all. I was serene, capable. Level-headed. I sorted my books by genre and then by author. I always made my bed in the morning. I never left dirty dishes in the sink. An orderly life was a happy life.

"How about you, then? You're obviously not from around here," I said after our plates had been removed for the next course.

"How about you guess where you think I'm from."

"The sixth level of hell," I deadpanned.

"My Catholic grandmama would agree, but I prefer the second level."

I remembered enough Dante from college to know which level that one was for: lust. The sixth was for heresy. I rolled my eyes. "Of course you would."

"I didn't grow up in hell, but close enough," said Liam, his accent lengthening. "I grew up in Ireland. Near Dublin, but I moved to the States when I was twenty."

So that was where his accent was from—no wonder I hadn't been able to place it. Sometimes it sounded pure Irish like right now, while other times it sounded almost American. I wondered if he tried to suppress his Irish accent just to avoid the inevitable *where are you from* questions. Which I'd just asked, I thought in dismay.

"I'd love to go to Ireland," I said. "I've never been out of the country. I was going to go to Paris this spring, but—" I could've bitten my tongue in half right then. I'd been planning a trip to Paris with David.

"But?" Liam prompted.

"Does it matter? It's not happening now."

"Don't get your feathers ruffled. It was only a simple question."

"My feathers have nothing to do with you."

Liam tipped his beer back, and I couldn't help but watch his Adam's apple bob as he swallowed. He even managed to drink beer suavely. Why couldn't he have the manners of a chimpanzee on a bender?

"So uptight," he said. His eyes sparkled. "I wonder what would happen if somebody could get you to unwind for once."

"Liam," interrupted Jenna, "we're so glad you were able to be Sam's best man. He didn't think you'd agree, but I knew that once I talked to you, you couldn't say no." Jenna looked toward me. "Liam hates weddings." Her eyes widened, like he'd told her he ran over puppies for fun.

"What do you have against weddings?" I said.

"What's the point of spending money on something that'll end within five years? Sounds like a waste of time to me."

"Wow, what a chip you have on your shoulder. How do you manage to walk around when it probably weighs five hundred pounds?"

Jenna clucked her tongue. "Mari, you won't convince him. He thinks love and romance and weddings are stupid. He's only here because Sam and I made him."

Strangely enough, despite David's betrayal, I still believed in love and romance and weddings. I still wanted all three. I didn't know if I'd ever get them now, though. I didn't know if I could let myself be vulnerable like that again. Maybe twenty years in the future. I'd enjoy the spinster life for now. I could get a cat or ten to keep me company. Really put in effort to be a true spinster.

I shot Liam a look, assessing him now that I knew one of his hang-ups. "So do you think love is just a fantasy?"

"Fantasy, hormones, load of bullshit. Whatever you want to call it."

"You don't love anyone, then?"

He just shrugged.

"No one. Not even Sam?"

"I'm not in love with the groom, no."

"That's not what I mean. You can love someone platonically. You mean you don't love your parents, or your friends, or—"

"What's with the inquisition? You're upset about something that has nothing to do with you."

Liam's cold, dead heart had nothing to do with me—he was right about that.

I was about to say as much when the ice sculpture began to collapse from the heat of the chandelier right above it.

The statue's butt had been melting and dripping onto a metal pan, sounding like faint rain, when suddenly, one of the statue's ankles gave way.

"Man down!" Mac hollered.

Liam jumped up only a second before the statue would've crashed into Laura's plate of mushroom risotto on the other side of me. Bridesmaids screamed; groomsmen swore. Liam caught the statue like it was a baby just in the nick of time, his jacket and shirt getting instantly soaked.

In the melee, a few glasses had been knocked over, and Jenna's mom had swooned at the end of the table. Waitstaff and employees hurried around us and apologized profusely.

"Will you take this damned thing?" growled Liam, still cradling the dripping statue.

"Of course, sir, so sorry, sir, this has never happened before, sir." A harried waiter took the statue, glanced in two different directions, and apparently decided to go into the kitchen with it.

In Liam's hand, though, was a piece of ice. A rather cylindrical piece that looked almost like—

"Oh my God." I said.

Liam held it up. "I'm holding a fucking cock, aren't I?"

"Looks like it." I was wheezing now.

Mac had come around to our side of the table. He slapped Liam on the shoulder as he passed us by. "Welcome to the club, my man."

CHAPTER THREE

LIAM

I hadn't planned to sleep with any women at Sam's wedding. Bridesmaids weren't my kink. They usually had their minds on marriage and had a bit of a chip on their shoulder because of the whole *always a bridesmaid, never a bride* bullshite.

The last time I'd fucked a bridesmaid she'd got drunk afterward and had cried over how her eight-year relationship with her boyfriend had ended and she'd die an old maid.

Nah, that wasn't my speed. Besides, it was the twenty-first century. Who gave a shite if they were married or not? You didn't need to put a ring on someone's finger to get awesome, sweaty sex with a willing partner.

I hadn't had awesome, sweaty sex in… I winced inwardly as I began to swim the next lap in the hotel pool. Way too fucking long. Three months, if I were being honest. My photography business had blown up. Which was great for my bank account, but not great for picking up chicks.

Right now I lived in Seattle, but I was dying to get the hell out of Dodge. I'd lived in so many places—Dublin, Los

Angeles, Atlanta, London, and now Seattle—that it felt strange to live in one place for more than one, maybe two, years.

Cities got stale. People got stale. Nothing about being tied down appealed to my wanderlust soul. The only reason I hadn't left Seattle sooner was that my little sister, Niamh, lived with our aunt and uncle in Olympia, two hours west of Seattle.

My sister was the one person who could get me to stick around. Once she turned eighteen and received her inheritance from our judgmental, conservative arse of a grandfather and started college, I wouldn't have to stick around. She'd be an adult on her own.

I'd always taken care of Niamh, even after she'd gone to live with our aunt and uncle.

I kicked off the wall, letting the warm water flow around me. I'd loved to swim ever since I was a kid living outside Dublin. I'd go to the community pool with Niamh every day during the summer, our mom always busy or not around. She always had to wear those bright orange floaties at the pool. She'd scream and cry when she'd first get into the pool, but she'd quickly ended up loving it.

Da had still been alive then. That first summer Niamh ever swam was the last one Da would be around for.

It was also only back in Ireland that people knew how to pronounce Niamh's name. Here in the States? Apparently that was too much to ask. I could hear Niamh in my mind saying to some stranger, "It's pronounced *Neev*," and then rolling her eyes when that person still mispronounced her name five minutes later.

I came up for air, slicking my hair back. It was late—close

to midnight. After the dinner tonight, I'd needed a breather from the wedding talk.

Then again, maybe I needed a second to cool off from meeting the one bridesmaid I'd be willing to fuck senseless.

Mari. It was too plain a name for someone as vibrant as her. Red hair, red lips. That dress she'd been wearing had been smoking hot. When she'd stood up after that statue fiasco, I'd also realized how tall she was. Slender legs that just begged to be wrapped around my waist.

As if I conjured her from my thoughts, Mari appeared. She came toward the pool, wearing a blue cover-up that failed to hide the string bikini underneath. Damn, she'd been hiding a body that was made for wet dreams under her dress tonight.

She stopped in surprise when she spotted me.

"You," she said accusingly. She crossed her arms across her chest. "What are you doing here?"

"What do you Americans say? 'It's a free country?'" I waved an arm. "Unless you're going to tell me the Irish have been banned from swimming in the hotel pool."

She rolled her eyes. "That's not what I meant. It's late, so I didn't think anyone would be here." She turned to leave, but for some stupid reason I didn't want her to. I lifted myself out of the pool, water streaming off of me. I couldn't help but grin when she eye-fucked me as I walked toward her.

Yeah, sue me. I wasn't against using this body of mine to get women to notice me. Women might act like looks didn't matter, but their own bodies betrayed them. Based on the way Mari's pupils had expanded, she wasn't immune to me.

Game, set, match.

If I didn't have Mari under me tonight, then I'd completely lost my touch.

So much for not sleeping with one of the bridesmaids, I thought.

"Why should you leave? You came here to swim. Or to get in the hot tub," I said.

She swallowed. "It's late," she repeated.

"Not that late. Besides, you're in Vegas. Time doesn't matter."

"How existential of you."

"You have no idea."

I raked my gaze down her body until I reached her toenails that were painted purple. I couldn't help but imagine what she'd look like behind the lens of my camera. Her skin peachy pink, her hair that deep red. Would she look at me like she was now, with a combination of wariness and lust? My body stirred at the thought, but I tamped it down.

As if something turned on inside her, Mari stepped back and walked around me. "I'm going for a swim," she said, so primly that I had the ridiculous desire to pull on her ponytail just to get a rise out of her.

"I'll race you."

She snorted. "Seriously?"

I waited for her to put on her swim cap and goggles. The combination of her bug eyes and bald head was almost enough to kill my horniness. Until she pulled off her swim cover-up to reveal that tiny bikini she was wearing.

I let out a whistle.

"Did you just wolf whistle?" she accused as she got into the pool next to me.

"Just appreciating what I see. Although the cap and goggles ain't too sexy, babe."

She gasped. "I'm no longer sexy to you? How shall I ever recover?"

I wanted to spank her for being such a smart-ass, but soon I was too caught up in winning this impromptu race with her. We soon agreed on ten laps.

The race began. She could swim, that was for sure. I hadn't expected her to be so fast. Her body was long and lean, and she gave as good as she got. By midway, she was ahead of me by one lap. When she turned, she flashed me a sassy grin and then dove below the surface again.

I pushed myself harder. Soon I'd caught up with her. By the last lap, we were neck and neck. My muscles screamed at me. My heart pounded.

And I touched the pool wall just a second before she did.

"Fuck yeah!" I burst through the water and slapped the pool ledge.

Mari wrinkled her nose and swiped the water from her face. She then lifted herself out of the water.

It was like something out of a magazine: the water streaming from her body, her swimsuit clinging to every curve, every dip. Her bikini bottom had ridden up, exposing the curves of her ass cheeks.

Hello, cockstand, nice to see you, but this was the *worst* fucking timing.

Mari took off her goggles and then her cap. Her red hair spilled free of its ponytail. Jesus fucking Christ, I wanted to wrap that hair around my fingers and pull it as I pumped into her from behind. Would she blush all over when she had sex?

I saw her shiver—it got cold at night in the desert—and I said, "Go get in the hot tub before you freeze."

She opened her mouth to argue, but then she considered my suggestion. I had a feeling she was the type to question everything. If I said the sky was blue, she'd probably ask me to prove it.

"Are you always so bossy with people you don't know?" she said.

"We know each other. I met you a few hours ago."

She rolled her eyes. "That doesn't—never mind."

She gave in and went to the hot tub, thank God. I didn't want her to leave yet. I climbed out of the pool to get into the hot tub with her.

Not next to her—that would spook her. If I pushed her too hard, she'd get her back up and scamper to her room and lock her door for all eternity.

"I didn't get in because you told me to," she said when I slid into the water across from her.

"I bet you're the one who bosses people around usually."

A smile tinged her lips. "You could say that. I also have two younger sisters, so I grew up bossing them around."

"Ah. I knew it. You have *oldest sister* written all over you."

"Really? What about you? Do you have siblings?"

"Just a younger sister."

"The worst kind." But her smile belied that statement. "So we're both bossy oldest siblings. No wonder I can't stand you."

I laughed. "Yet you haven't left."

"No," she said softly, "I haven't."

The steam had made the ends of her hair curl, especially around her forehead. I wished I had my camera right then. In the one art class I managed to take in college before I dropped out, we studied the Romantics, including Rossetti's obsession with his titian-haired muse.

Mari looked like she could be one of Rossetti's paintings. It was such a romantic thought that I cringed inwardly. *She's not going to be your muse. Just a one-night stand, unless you totally fuck this up.*

"How did you meet Sam?" said Mari suddenly. "You guys don't seem like you'd have much in common."

"And you've figured that out from knowing me for—what? —four hours?"

"I'm very astute. I usually figure people out quickly."

I swam toward her until we sat next to each other. I could touch her if I reached for her, but I didn't. There was something to be said about anticipation. Her eyes widened slightly, her nostrils flared.

She was like a pretty filly that would bolt if I moved too quickly. In Ireland, we'd lived next to a farm that'd had horses, and I'd helped the owner with mucking the stables and feeding the horses when I was a kid.

I had a feeling Mari wouldn't appreciate me comparing her to a horse, though.

"So you're saying you're a mind reader?" I said.

"No. But most people operate based on their own kind of logic. Once you know their mode of operation, you can anticipate what they'll say and do. Generally speaking."

"People aren't machines."

"No, but they are predictable."

"What a boring outlook you have of humanity."

She wrinkled her pert little nose. Although the lights were dim, I could make out freckles on her cheeks.

"I find it comforting," she asserted. "That people can be figured out easily. Then you can avoid the ones who'll hurt you."

"If people are so simple," I said, my voice low as I moved

closer to her, "then tell me what I'm going to do right now. What is my standard mode of operation?"

She took a deep breath. Her breasts rose and fell, and I could see that her nipples were hard. It would be so easy to untie those few strings holding the scrap of fabric on her.

"You're going to touch me," she whispered.

I shook my head. "Believe me, I'd like to. But you're not ready. You'd enjoy it in the moment, but then you'd remember why it was a bad idea. Because you don't like to do bad things, do you? You're a good girl, Mari."

"You think you have me all figured out."

I shrugged. "Like you said: people are easy to understand."

"I do bad things all the time," she countered.

"I doubt it."

She tipped her pointed chin up. "I'm not a coward."

"Maybe not, but you do prefer to stay where it's safe. Tell me I'm wrong."

Her cheeks, already flushed from the steam, then got even redder at my words. Mari was right, in a way: people were simple to figure out. She hated being proven wrong, I could already tell.

"You're wrong," she hissed, and I laughed.

Then she launched herself at me. My laughter died in my throat when her hot body wrapped around me right before her mouth descended onto mine.

She kissed artlessly, like she hadn't much experience. Or she'd only kissed a man bad at kissing. I let her control the kiss for three seconds, letting her believe she'd won.

Then I turned the tables on her.

I slid my hands down her back and squeezed her arse as I thrust my tongue into her mouth. She gasped, her hands fluttering on my shoulders. I fucked her mouth—that was the only way to describe it. And she was fire in my arms. She trembled and dug her nails into my skin. She arched toward me when I slid my finger under the string of her bikini tie around her neck.

I was close to untying this entire bikini from her body and feasting on her when I heard footsteps.

I didn't know who reacted first, me or Mari. One second she was in my arms. The next, water was splashing over the side of the hot tub as Mari jumped away from me. Unfortunately for her, I was still gripping the end of her string bikini top. The string un-knotted in slow motion, and then the bikini folded over to reveal her breasts.

Mari screeched. I tried to help her, but she scrambled out of the hot tub before I could reach her.

"Well, damn. I should've come down here earlier," our visitor said.

"Mari, wait." I went after her as fast as I could, considering the slick pavement. She grabbed her stuff, holding her bikini top up with one hand.

"You've done more than enough. Leave me alone," she said, obviously pissed.

And then she left in a huff, scampering back to her room, just like I'd predicted.

At least I'd got to see her amazing tits. I should've felt guilty thinking about them—flushed from the steam, berry-pink nipples—but I was a man with a working cock.

Shame I'd probably never get a chance to see them again.

CHAPTER FOUR

MARI

When the exotic dancer Laura had hired began to give me a lap dance, I almost fell backward out of my seat. My fellow bridesmaids hooted and hollered like a bunch of men at a cheap strip joint. I'd neglected to bring any dollar bills, but Jenna had handed me a stack with a wide grin before the party had started.

"Yeah, get up on her!" yelled Reagan. She was the youngest of the bridesmaids, and she always seemed to have a flask of booze on hand at every occasion. Breakfast: vodka in her coffee; lunch, gin in her Coke; dinner, straight rum. Yet she always seemed perfectly sober. I didn't know whether to be concerned or impressed.

"Shake it!" Jenna screamed as the exotic dancer shimmied and turned to give me a view of his bare ass covered only by a gold G-string. It was so perfectly smooth I was tempted to ask him how he'd done it. Wax? Sugaring? Laser? It was like he'd never had a single hair on his butt ever.

The dancer turned around, smiling widely, his crotch dangerously close to my face. If he moved in the wrong direction, his penis would be slapping me in the face. How awkward would that be? *Woman receives black eye after she's slapped in the face with dancer's penis*, the headline would read.

I grabbed a few dollars and put them in the dancer's waistband that was barely a band at all. I was half-afraid it'd snap and reveal the guy's pretty substantial package right then and there.

"Thanks, babe." He winked and moved on to Reagan. I let out a breath of relief and fanned myself.

"Are you having fun?" Jenna yelled the words into my ear.

We'd been at her bachelorette party for two hours now, and everyone was pretty wasted already. I'd been nursing my cocktail; I didn't want to go to bed drunk and wake up hungover for Jenna's wedding. I didn't know how Jenna would survive tomorrow if she kept drinking, but that was her choice, not mine.

I was a good girl. Except for that whole kissing a strange man in a hot tub thing last night. And then accidentally flashing my boobs at him and another man.

I'd decided to forget that had even happened. It had been a moment of insanity and nothing more. It would just be one of those "what happens in Vegas stays in Vegas" moments that I'd remember briefly when I was in a nursing home, sighing over my misbegotten youth.

Thank God the guys had been together for the bachelor party: I hadn't seen Liam at all. The last thing I needed was him goading me into kissing him again. Or reminding me that he'd seen my breasts. God, that had been so humiliating!

"Loads of fun!" I lied to Jenna. "That guy is something."

"Isn't he? I wouldn't kick him out of my bed." Jenna sighed happily. "Sam gave me a lap dance once, but it was so awkward. He tripped over my feet and ended up face planting into my lap."

"Oh my God, Jenna."

"He got a bloody nose and everything. Had to lie to his buddies at work that he'd gotten into a fight when his nose was all purple." Jenna giggled. "Don't tell anyone I told you that! He'd kill me."

I checked my phone, wondering if I could bounce early, when I very stupidly looked on Facebook. I'd unfriended David months ago, but we had a bunch of mutual friends, so I still saw his public posts all the time. The blood drained from my face when I saw that he was now officially in a relationship with the woman I'd caught him screwing in our bed.

I wasn't surprised, but the fact that so many people were commenting positively, congratulating them both, made me want to vomit up my cocktail. He could at least be *discreet*, for God's sake.

I couldn't help myself when I clicked on his updated profile photo of him and his new girlfriend, Samantha. They looked so happy. He had his arm around her, and she was kissing his cheek. Like neither of them had done anything wrong. Rage burned through me.

"You want another drink?" said the waitress.

My plans not to drink flew right out the window within two seconds. I wanted to forget, and I wanted to have some fun for once. I was tired of being responsible when it didn't seem to make a difference anyway. What did it matter if I just ended up showing my breasts to strange men anyway?

"Yes. A round of shots for everyone, actually," I said.

The first shot made my blood hum pleasantly. The second, the same. By the third, the exotic dancer gave me another lap dance, and I was hooting and hollering with everyone else. He was so hot.

I swallowed a fourth shot after I'd tipped him generously, very tempted to stuff those dollar bills in the pouch covering his package.

"It's time for the party favors!" Laura brought out the box of pink bags and began handing them out. "Jenna, we wanted you to have lots of fun on your honeymoon." Laura winked.

Jenna began throwing tissue paper out of her bag and then screeched when she pulled out a huge pink dildo. "You bitch!" she said as she laughed. "Oh my God, what else is in here?"

In quick succession, we all discovered that we'd received dildos, butt plugs, bullet vibes, and a strip of condoms. Oh, and cherry-flavored lube, of course.

Reagan squeezed a dollop of the lube onto her tongue and then promptly spit it out. "It tastes like cough syrup!"

"Still probably tastes better than dick," said Nina, Jenna's cousin.

"What kind of dick you sucking on? I'm concerned." This from Reagan.

Nina had recently gotten divorced and hated men more than me. She wrinkled her nose. "Don't act like sucking on a dick is enjoyable."

Laura shrugged. "It's fun when they're super into it."

"Do you guys swallow or spit?" said Reagan.

Everyone's answers varied. I drank my latest cocktail, hoping no one would notice I wasn't answering.

"Mari, what about you? Spit or swallow?" said Jenna.

The alcohol made my tongue loose and lying didn't even

come into my brain. "I don't know. I've never given a blowjob."

The entire group stared at me like I'd admitted to enjoying having sex with furries.

Finally Reagan sputtered, "Are you serious? Weren't you engaged?"

Jenna elbowed Reagan, but I was too drunk to care about someone mentioning David. I shrugged. "David never wanted one, and he was my only real boyfriend."

"Did he go down on you?" This from Laura.

"No. We didn't do oral, period."

Everyone went crazy when I admitted that, and it only made me want to drink further. Questions were volleyed like balls, back and forth, and eventually I was forgotten in the rousing discussion.

So what if my sex life had always been vanilla? I was fine with that. I didn't need some guy to spank me and make me wear a butt plug to feel fulfilled.

Of course, my mind drifted to last night at the pool. Considering I'd launched myself at Liam, mauled him, and had kissed him like I was dying, I was obviously not just into vanilla sex. Or at least vanilla kissing.

Maybe I needed Liam to spank me while I wore a butt plug. I'd get it out of my system and return to missionary sex during commercial breaks like I'd had with David.

Could I ask him if he'd want to? I was so drunk it didn't seem like a terrible idea. Besides, Liam seemed like he'd be into anything that related to sex. He'd probably grin and pull out his own butt plug he'd had specially made for just those moments.

"No wonder you broke up with him," said Reagan as she

slung an arm across my shoulders. "The shitty sex should've been a red flag."

I bristled. "You don't know what you're talking about."

"Don't get defensive. We've all been there."

Suddenly, the room felt too close, too hot. I slid out from Reagan's arm and staggered outside into the cool night air. I expected someone to follow me, but they were probably too wasted right now to notice my departure.

I inhaled deep breaths. Panic spiraled in my gut for some strange reason. I felt dizzy. I'd obviously drunk way too much. Geez, I was an idiot.

The lights of the Vegas strip lit up the town, making it seem like it was almost midday even though the sun had set hours ago. People walked up and down the sidewalk, some clearly drunk, others laughing and yelling. A cop took one man aside when he tried to pee in a trashcan nearby; another woman proceeded to lie down on a bench and take a nap, her friend pulling on her arm and whining about needing to get back to their hotel.

"You okay?"

I blinked to see Liam standing over me. And if I wasn't mistaken he seemed…concerned. Maybe I was hallucinating now.

"I'm fine." I tried to step away from him, but I only proceeded to almost fall flat on my face.

"Whoa there. How much have you had to drink?" He caught my elbow and propped me against the wall, searching my face. "Where's everyone else?"

I yawned. "Inside. I'm fine."

"You're rat-arsed."

"I don't even know what that means."

"It means you're shit-faced."

"Well, your face is shit." I snort-laughed at that insult.

"Yes, very rat-arsed. Come on, I'm taking you back to the hotel."

The thought of sitting in my room, alone, thinking about David and his stupid new girlfriend, made me panic. It would be unbearable, and since I was drunk I'd end up doing something stupid, like call him. Or cry. Or sit up watching infomercials and crying because David had been obsessed with his ShamWow.

"I don't want to. Let's go somewhere. I've barely seen Vegas at all." I widened my eyes. "Oh my God, wait!"

"Wait? Why?"

"You saw my boobs!"

Liam chuckled, a sound like warm whiskey through my veins. "Yeah, I did."

"I can't hang out with you now."

"If it makes you feel better, your tits are gorgeous."

I was drunk enough to preen under the compliment. "Okay. You're forgiven. Now, let's go somewhere."

Liam frowned down at me, though. "You can hardly walk."

"Then you can carry me."

He smiled, brushed some stray strands of hair from my forehead, and took my arm. "Stay here," he said as he left me inside the entrance of the club.

He returned a few minutes later. I'd gotten bored and had begun to count the number of diamonds in the carpet.

"There are ten on this side, but eleven over here. Isn't that weird?" I pointed at the hostess. "Have you noticed that?"

"I have not," she said seriously. "We appreciate the feedback, though."

"I'm going to file a complaint online. Your carpet is totally weird!"

Liam hauled me outside. "Behave yourself."

"Or what?" I grinned up at him. "You'll spank me?"

Instead of rolling his eyes, he growled, "Don't tempt me."

Well, that answered one part of my question. I was close to asking him if he had his own special butt plug when we arrived at a casino combined with a restaurant that buzzed with activity.

"We're sobering you up with some food," he said.

"No! I don't want to be sober!" I grasped his arm. "Because then I'll just think about *him*—"

Liam's eyes flashed, but it could have been the bright lights overhead making me see things.

"When's the last time you got this rat-arsed?" he said.

It wasn't the question I was expecting. "I don't know —college?"

"Mari—"

"Does it matter? I don't want to be sober. I want to do fun things and not think for once. Can you do that for me tonight?" I batted my eyelashes. "Please?"

He sighed, but he didn't talk about getting me sober a second time. Before I knew it, we were drinking and gambling the night away.

When I sat at a slot machine, feeding it quarters like an infinitely hungry Pac-Man, Liam whispered in my ear, "Who is the guy you can't stop thinking about?"

I pulled the lever. I'd only won a few hundred dollars so far, but I couldn't remember how much I'd spent. There was an infinite amount of quarters at my disposal, it seemed, so it didn't matter.

I didn't win this time. I grabbed some more coins.

"Mari," said Liam more firmly.

Heat scorched my cheeks, most likely from the amount of alcohol in my system. I tended to get flushed and sweaty when I was drunk. Or maybe it was Liam's close proximity that made my heart skip a beat and beads of sweat to form on my forehead.

"I don't know who you mean," I said in a high-pitched voice. I slammed a quarter into one of the slots. "I don't like men. At all. They suck."

Liam leaned against the machine next to me. "You know when you lie, you don't look people in the eye?"

I swiveled to face him, only to get dizzy. I grabbed onto my seat to keep from toppling over like a drunken doll.

"Are *you* drunk?" I said to him.

I couldn't tell. He'd been drinking as much as me, but he wasn't flushed, or sweaty, or falling out of his chair. It was annoying.

"I'm not sober," he conceded.

"Can't you ever answer a question with a straight answer? You hurt my brain."

"You're the one avoiding my question."

I chewed on the inside of my cheek. Who cared if Liam knew? I'd never see him again after Jenna's wedding, and he was probably too drunk to remember. Or wouldn't care about remembering the weird chick who'd begged him to hang out with her in a casino.

I said, "My fiancé cheated on me six months ago. Now he's in a relationship with the chick he cheated on me with.

It's all over Facebook. Her name is Samantha, because she's a total cliché. Do men never cheat on women with chicks named Susan or Deborah? No, they're always Brittany or Tiffany or Samantha."

"Probably because Susan and Deborah are both sixty-five," said Liam rather gently.

I waved away his logical explanation. "David cheated on me. I don't want to think about it anymore. So I'm going to win this slot machine and you're going to stop asking me questions."

I pulled the lever, but I didn't win. I sighed.

"You know what I think?" Liam now stood over my shoulder. His breath was hot against my cheek.

I froze. I felt that kiss from last night, and I wished we were back in the hot tub together.

"That fiancé of yours didn't deserve you. No man with half a brain would cheat on a woman like you." He pushed my hair aside to bare my neck; his lips traced a line down to my shoulder. "Then again, I'm not sad he cheated on you."

My spine stiffened. "Excuse me?"

"Because then you'd be off-limits otherwise." He nipped my neck. "I don't go after other dudes' girls. It's his loss, darling."

My brain felt sloshy, and my heart felt squishy. I wanted Liam to keep kissing me, even though a tiny voice inside my head whispered, *bad idea, bad idea, danger, DANGER.* I snuffed out that little voice. I didn't need to be good girl Mari tonight.

I turned to face Liam. "I want to do something with you," I blurted.

He smiled. "Anything specific?"

In for a penny, in for a pound. "Yes. Sex. Sexual things. Kinky things. Do you like butt plugs?"

Apparently I spoke so loudly that the people around us heard me. Liam covered my mouth, gasping as he laughed, but he still hadn't answered yes or no.

"Mari, darling, you're very drunk—"

"As drunk as you are."

"Doubtful." He lowered his voice. "As much as I would love to play with your arse, I think we should start slowly. Don't you?"

"You sound like a virgin. Don't you want me, Liam?" I pouted.

He swore under his breath and proceeded to drink his tumbler of whiskey in one gulp.

"God, I'm a fucking cliché," he muttered. "Come on. We're winning some money tonight."

The night passed in a blur of colors and alcohol. We played blackjack, which was the only card game I knew how to play, and I won a few hundred dollars. I then watched Liam play; despite the buzz from the whiskey he was drinking, he was a fierce card player. He ended up walking away with a cool five thousand.

I couldn't remember how we ended up outside, or how I ended up pressed against the wall with Liam pinning me there. I didn't think about how it was probably a bad idea that we were making out in public, even if it was dark.

"I want to do bad things to you," he said, his brogue more noticeable now. "You're so sweet and innocent."

"I'm not a virgin."

"You can not be a virgin and still be innocent." He hooked my leg over his hip, grinding his erection against my aching pussy. If he kept that up, I'd come right here in some alley in Las Vegas. And strangely enough, I didn't even care.

"You're exactly what I didn't need right now." Liam kissed me hard. Plunging his tongue inside my mouth, I gasped and squirmed. I needed him to press his cock against my clit. I needed to dry hump him until the itch inside me went away.

I didn't know where the idea came from. One moment I was kissing Liam, the next he was saying, "Let's get married."

What could I say? I was drunk. It sounded like a great idea. And David would *hate* it. Two birds, one stone: the perfect plan where nothing could possibly go wrong.

CHAPTER FIVE

MARI

Present day

On the list of things I thought I'd never do, walking down the aisle arm-in-arm with my secret husband at my best friend's wedding was not one of them.

"You're walking too fast," I hissed at Liam.

"Why are you going so slowly?" he snapped back.

I wanted to lob him over the head with my bouquet, but I couldn't imagine Jenna and Sam would appreciate a brawl in the middle of their ceremony. I put on a tight smile as Liam and I approached the front of the chapel.

Jenna and Sam had chosen one of those chapels that looks like it was built in the Middle Ages, with vaulted ceilings, stained glass windows, and an actual altar at the front. Since this was Las Vegas, it was actually built only twenty years ago. Behind the chapel was a reception room that boasted everything from a huge parquet dance floor to a stripper pole in the corner, along with plenty of dark corners to drunkenly make out with however many wedding guests you wanted.

After I'd rushed out of my hotel room this morning, I'd finally looked at my phone to see a bunch of texts and missed calls from my sister Dani. Apparently I'd texted her about Liam last night. Great, just great. So much for keeping this a secret.

You need to call me, the last text had read. *I'm freaking out. I won't tell Mom and Dad but if you don't call me soon I'll come down to Vegas myself.*

I'd sent my sister a quick text before my hair appointment this morning.

I'm fine. Well, sort of. I'm getting my hair done. I'm safe. Don't tell anyone, okay? I'm still figuring things out.

Dani had told me to call her as soon as I could. But what could I say? I didn't know exactly how this had happened to begin with. My memories were a jumbled mess.

Now hours later, the wedding was about to begin. My head still hurt from this morning despite all of the ibuprofen I'd taken. I wanted to attribute it to how tightly the hair stylist had pulled my hair into its current braid-bun concoction.

To add to my discomfort, my dress was heavy green satin but tight through the torso until it fanned out in a mermaid style. I was so tightly bound with Spanx and hosiery I was rather afraid I'd burst out of my dress like the Hulk if I bent over.

A second before Liam and I parted ways, he whispered in my ear, "Your arse looks amazing in that dress."

I knew he'd said it just to rile me, knowing I couldn't say anything back. He grinned as he went to stand by Sam and the rest of the groomsmen.

In a tux, Liam was devastating: the white of his dress shirt made his hair seem pitch-black. The way he filled out his coat, the green of his bow tie, the way his collar brushed his jaw—he put the rest of the men to shame. Even Sam, who looked as dapper as I'd ever seen him, couldn't compete with Liam Gallagher.

"All rise," said the officiant. Instantly, I was distracted as Jenna walked down the aisle with her father. Tears sprang to my eyes.

I should be married already, I thought, only to remember I *was* married. Just to the wrong man.

David and I were supposed to have gotten married two months ago. I should've been called the unflattering matron of honor at this wedding. David should've been sitting on the bride's side of the chapel, smiling up at me, reminding me of *our* wedding. How we'd have a life of love and happiness together forever.

That life with David would never happen now. And now I was married to a man I didn't know. I didn't know how old he was, or his favorite color, or if he liked cream in his coffee. All the tiny details you're supposed to know about a person before you marry them.

As if he could read my thoughts, Liam caught my gaze. He didn't break eye contact throughout the exchange of vows. The sound of them forced more memories into my brain from the night before.

I could almost feel Liam's hand as he put that ring pop on my finger. I could hear how deep and rough his voice was as he'd said *his* vows. Except last night we'd chosen the *Princess Bride* priest impersonator as our officiant. I remembered that now because Liam hadn't understood why I'd thought it was so hilarious.

Haven't you ever seen the movie? I'd demanded.

Why would I have watched a movie called The Princess Bride? he'd countered.

The impersonator had done the entire speech like the one in the movie, and I could hear the mispronunciation of marriage in my brain as Jenna and Sam vowed to love and to cherish each other for always.

Mawiage is what bwings us together, todaaaay.

I had to bite the inside of my cheek right then to keep from laughing.

I was so distracted that I nearly jumped out of my skin when the audience started clapping. Sam dipped Jenna over his arm and gave her a loud, smacking kiss.

Soon, I was once again on Liam's arm.

"What was so funny?" he murmured. "You looked like you were going to lose it."

"I was not."

"You really love telling me I'm wrong."

I scowled up at him and pinched the skin near his bare wrist hard enough that he winced. "Behave yourself tonight. I grew up with crazy parents who owned a flower shop. I know which plants can kill you."

"Good thing we're in a desert," he drawled.

The rest of the evening became a blur. There was a cocktail hour, where I sipped on a martini for the better part of two hours, conscious of how much I'd had to drink last night. My poor liver needed a break.

I also avoided Liam as much as I could. When he started walking toward me on two different occasions, I bolted each time. Once to a nearby table filled with the groom's grandparents, who all told me I looked cold in my dress and should put on a sweater. The other time I hid behind a waiter, following him almost to the kitchen before he'd asked in confusion what the hell I was doing.

"Mariiiiiiiii!" Jenna slung her arm around my shoulder as she lifted her wineglass to the ceiling. "I'm soooooooo glad you came! I wasn't sure if you would!"

"Of course I came. Why wouldn't I?"

Jenna frowned, her bottom lip protruding. Based on the flush in her cheeks and the way her hair was already falling down, she'd had her fair share of cocktails.

"The whole David thing. I didn't know if you'd want to come to my wedding. If Sam had done that to me—" She shuddered. "I'd be in jail after I murdered him!" She let out a peal of laughter that made me wince.

Jenna was normally more circumspect than this, but alcohol tended to turn her into a combination of overly opinionated and touchy-feely. She caressed my arm like I was a cat.

"I wouldn't have missed your wedding," I said sincerely. "Besides, I needed to get out of town."

"I don't blame you. I'd never go back after what happened." Jenna clucked her tongue and patted my cheek. "Poor Mari. I thought you'd be the first of us to get married, but here we are."

Poor Mari. I'd been hearing that a lot lately.

Poor Mari, her fiancé cheated on her. Poor Mari, her wedding got called off. Poor Mari, she always had her life together, didn't she? Until now.

I downed the rest of my martini in one gulp.

"Are you avoiding me?" a male voice said over my shoulder.

I didn't need to turn to know who it was. "Of course I

am," I said. "Who would want to keep looking their biggest mistake in the face?"

"So that's what you do? Avoid the hard things in life?"

His accent caressed the word *hard*, and I knew very well he meant himself in more ways than one.

"Hard things only get me into trouble," I said. "Why go after things that make your life more complicated?"

"Because sometimes the hardest things can bring the most pleasure."

I could feel the heat of him behind me. If he stepped an inch closer, he'd be pressed against the length of my back. The image of his naked cock this morning flashed in my memory, and my nipples hardened to peaks, the traitors. At least Liam couldn't see how turned on I was simply from the timbre of his voice.

Liam made me turn toward him, and he smiled as he saw my nipples pressing against the satin of my dress.

"You seem a little wound up, wife. I could always help you with that."

Right as he said those words, one of the groomsmen passed by us. I held my breath, wondering if he'd heard anything. Based on how enthusiastically he was eating his shrimp cocktail, he hadn't overheard.

"Will you shut up? Do you want everyone to find out what happened?"

Liam tapped his chin. "What will you give me, if I keep quiet?"

I stared at him in surprise. Was he seriously *blackmailing* me? I wanted to stab him with a cocktail fork. At this point, I didn't care if I ruined Jenna's wedding. Getting hauled out by the police would be the least of my worries.

"I don't have any money," I said, because it was true. My savings had been used for my now-canceled wedding. Most of the deposits had been nonrefundable after a certain point as well.

"I don't need money," he said coolly.

I lifted my chin. "I'm not sleeping with you."

"I don't need to pay for sex." He sounded almost offended, which mollified me slightly.

But we were quickly interrupted when Laura broke our tête-à-tête to tell us everyone was heading to the reception.

I wanted to hug her for ending that bizarre conversation. I just hoped Liam had been bluffing, otherwise I was in trouble.

My phone buzzed in my clutch. Slipping away into a mostly deserted hallway, I girded my loins and answered my sister's call.

"Mari! Oh my God, how could you not call me hours ago?" Dani sounded genuinely upset. I instantly felt guilty.

"I'm sorry. I had to do all this wedding stuff, plus the ceremony itself—"

"I don't care about Jenna's wedding. I care about *yours*. What the hell happened last night? Are you okay?"

I assured her that I was okay and not locked up in some casino dungeon. I went so far as to text her a photo of me in the hallway, no handcuffs or ropes or chains on me. I'd made this metaphorical dungeon on my own.

"You don't remember the ceremony itself?" said Dani.

I chewed on my bottom lip before remembering that would smudge my lipstick and get it all over my teeth. I might be in a mess, but it didn't mean I had to *look* like a mess.

"I'm remembering more and more. I didn't this morning, but it's coming back to me in fits and starts." I sighed deeply.

"Honestly, I think I just blocked it from my mind this morning because I was so freaked out."

I heard a man's voice on the phone—Dani's boyfriend, Jacob. Dani said something to him before saying to me, "Jacob says he tried to do some research on Liam Gallagher, but there were way too many in Seattle and the surrounding area. He needs more details."

"Sorry, I don't have his social security or birthdate on hand," I said sarcastically.

"Then you should get both. You need to make sure he isn't some serial killer."

"Who gets married to somebody they're going to murder? That seems like a waste of time. Plus, 'serial killer' isn't going to come up on a background check."

"At least you'd know something about him. And are we really debating how *logical* any of this is? You just drunk-married some stranger in Vegas. Logic flew out the window ages ago."

I sighed. "Look, I don't think he's a bad guy—"

"How would you know? You know nothing about him!"

"He is Sam's best friend…" Still, how did I know? And wasn't I being stupid, considering Liam had just tried to blackmail me less than an hour ago? Okay, so maybe he wasn't the *best* man, pun intended. That didn't mean I felt like I was in danger-danger.

"You need to make sure he isn't using you for something," said Dani.

"Like what? He's the mob boss of Seattle or something?"

"He could be a criminal. You never know. Why would he marry some woman out of the blue?"

"Because we were both drunk and dumb? Besides, I'm

hardly a great person to marry. I don't have any money, so if we have to divorce instead of get an annulment, he won't get much of anything."

Dani let out a breath. "Okay, you have a point. If he is a criminal, he's a bad one. You're a terrible mark."

"Thank you?"

"Although he could have a lair in the Seattle underground. Keeps virgins and the heads of his victims down there."

"Yeah, I'm sure the tour guides going down there would've noticed a bunch of decomposing heads, Dani."

"Jacob says he knows a good lawyer who can get your marriage annulled quickly. He even called him this morning."

I smiled, even though my heart hurt a little, hearing how happy my sister was. She deserved a good man who adored her, and despite a rocky beginning, she and Jacob were almost disgustingly happy together now.

He and his family actually owned the rival flower shop that was currently merging with our family's shop, Buds and Blossoms. Dani had taken over Buds and Blossoms a few years ago after my parents had retired. She'd always been the one good with plants. I was decent with them, but I wasn't obsessed with them like Dani. Our younger sister Kate, though, was the one with the black thumb. Any plant she touched withered and died.

"Tell Jacob thanks," I said. "I have to get back to the reception."

After Dani asked me to send her photos of the floral centerpieces since she loved to find inspiration from other designers, she told me to stay safe and not do anything stupider than marrying some random stranger.

It was strange that I was the misbehaving sister right now.

I'd always been the good one. Dani had been the oddball, with plants in her backpack when she went to school, while Kate had been the one my parents despaired over. Not only could she not grow the easiest type of fern that literally needed zero watering, but she was impulsive and always got into trouble. She still managed to get into trouble now despite being almost twenty.

I didn't want to be the bad girl. Bad girls always got punished. The feeling that I'd stepped out of line and would face dire consequences made my gut churn with anxiety. Jenna's wedding had provided enough of a distraction to keep my anxiety at bay, but now it washed over me in full force.

I wrapped my arms around my middle, taking deep breaths. I felt that prickling of my skin that signaled I was about to get light-headed. Before I knew it, I was sliding down the wall and sitting on the floor with my head between my knees.

I took slow, deep breaths. I knew, objectively, that this was a panic attack, but it only helped soothe my pounding heart a little. I hadn't felt this panicky in a long time. Not since I was a kid and my parents had been struggling to keep everything together. When I'd felt like I needed to be good just to keep everyone I loved happy and safe.

The panic abated. When the light-headedness faded, I forced myself to stand and go to the reception with a smile on my face.

CHAPTER SIX

LIAM

My new wife was avoiding me.

I watched her dance during the reception, her green dress tight against her curves. One of the groomsmen— Kevin? Keith?—had his hands dangerously close to her arse. One more inch and he'd have a nice handful.

Mari, to her credit, somehow managed to wiggle out of his grip to move his hands to a more appropriate place on her back without missing a beat. It was only her smile faltering that showed she was annoyed.

I'd got good at reading my wife in the last two days.

My wife. My bloody fucking wife.

Me, the guy who hated the idea of marriage. I was a bitter old man in a young man's body when it came to shite like this. Yet I'd skipped to the altar like a starry-eyed girl the second I got rat-arsed and horny for a gorgeous redhead.

It'll make me feel better, she'd said, her cheeks flushed, her eyes glassy. *It'll make David so mad. And it'd be fun. Don't you like to have fun?*

I liked to have fun. Fun that didn't involve signing my life away to a woman in one fell swoop.

I didn't have the excuse that I'd been too drunk to consent. Unlike Mari, I had a high alcohol tolerance. My mind had warned me that the idea was ludicrous. But it'd been easy to blame the booze.

The booze made me stand in front of a lisping minister wearing a cheap robe that had seen better days. Our witnesses had been a man wearing black with a sword strapped to his side and another man who kept saying *Inconceivable!* after the ceremony. Mari had thought all of it was hilarious, especially as she'd tried to explain the plot of *The Princess Bride* while totally smashed.

I'd told myself at the time the booze had made me sign my name on that license. The booze had made me think it would be a grand idea. Besides, she'd said she'd wanted to do it to get back at her ex, and somehow that had appealed to me.

I married the girl you were too fucking stupid to keep for yourself.

Yet now, in the cold light of day, I could only think: what the fuck was I going to do now?

My attention was caught by that damn groomsman, who had his hands back on Mari's arse. Jesus Christ, I'd had enough of this.

"My turn," I said, right as the song ended. Keith-Kevin-whoever opened his mouth to protest, but I didn't wait for him to speak. I took Mari into my arms and whirled her away.

"That was rude," she complained.

I stared at her. "I was *saving* you."

"I can take care of myself."

"He had his hands practically up your arse."

Mari's lips pursed. She had this expression—like a prim

schoolteacher—that made me want to take her hair down and make her messy. Begging for me, crying out my name. I had a feeling it wouldn't take much to get my prissy wife to become a total demon in the sack. She was so wound up, so concerned about what other people thought, that she was the type of woman who needed more than just the physical release of sex.

You sound like a goddamn shrink, I thought.

"How would he have gotten his hands *up* my butt? I'm wearing a dress and so much Spanx I can barely breathe. Honestly, if he managed that, I'd give him a medal."

"If you keep talking about this other guy, wife, I'm taking you upstairs."

I breathed the words into her ear, although the music was so loud nobody would've heard me. But I knew she was antsy about me blabbing about our wedding. I'd been bluffing—I didn't need anyone knowing about it, either.

Keeping Mari on her toes, however? Worth the little white lie.

Logically, there was no reason to keep her on the hook. I didn't want marriage or a wife. Yet somehow I already felt like she was mine to protect. Mine to savor. It was a primal, unreasonable feeling that I didn't want to examine too much. Or maybe it was just that Mari was so resistant to the idea that I wanted to make her change her mind.

"I'm not your wife," said Mari in that crisp schoolteacher voice.

Speak of the devil...

"Did you already forget what we did last night?"

"A drunken ceremony in Vegas doesn't make us actual spouses. Even you can understand that."

I twirled her around and when she returned to my arms, I

let one of my hands drift down her back until it settled right above her arse. One I was keen to make mine, along with the rest of her body.

"Yet your nipples are as hard as diamonds, and you're all flushed. Every time you get near me you're aroused. I bet those Spanx of yours are soaked right now."

She scowled. "You're annoying. And that's hardly a sexy image, you know."

"Ripping you out of them is pretty sexy, though."

"I'd love to see you try. These things are like elastic armor."

"Challenge accepted."

Her eyes flashed, her lips twitching at the corners. I dipped her again, enjoying the flash of her cleavage. What a fucking shame that we'd been too smashed last night to fuck.

"I think you married me last night because you wanted a real man for once," I said quietly. "One who wasn't afraid of you."

"Now you think you know me."

"What did you say two nights ago? That people were easy to figure out?"

"So you've already figured me out."

"I'm getting there."

Mari's smile had disappeared. Once the song ended, she pushed away from me and walked off.

I wasn't disappointed at her leaving; it just gave me an opportunity to watch her hips sway as she walked in those heels.

"What was that all about?" said Sam at my elbow once I'd returned to the reception table. "Mari looked pissed."

"Doesn't she always?"

"Mari? No. I don't think I've ever seen her angry. She's always pretty cheerful." Sam frowned at me. "Gallagher, I told you to leave the bridesmaids alone. You're not screwing around with Mari, are you?"

I almost choked. Christ, Sam would kill me if he found out what we'd done last night. "She practically has an ironclad chastity belt around her. I'd probably lose a hand trying." It was only half a lie.

Sam looked a little mollified. "She was really messed up when her fiancé—well, just don't be an ass. She's been through enough."

I looked around for my wife, but Mari must've left the reception entirely. I considered going after her. But why bother when she was pissy?

Instead, I danced with a few more of the bridesmaids to pass the time. One of them, Reagan, was giving me such obvious signals that she was interested that I was halfway tempted to take her up on the invitation. It wasn't like my wife would welcome me into her bed tonight.

"You're from Ireland?" Reagan's eyes widened exaggeratedly. "No wonder your accent is so sexy."

Subtle, this one. "I've been in the States for a while now."

"I've always wanted to go to London. Isn't the queen there? I wanted to marry Prince William when I was younger." Reagan giggled.

My Irish side bristled, but Americans weren't known for understanding the history of Ireland and the United Kingdom. They thought it was all the same country, for Christ's sake. I'd been amazed when I'd met an American who'd actually known Ireland and Northern Ireland were two separate countries.

"Do you speak—oh, what is it called—"

"Gaelic?" I said gently. "Irish is fine, too."

Reagan lit up. "Yes! Like Jamie from *Outlander*. If you speak it, I'll probably burst into flames. It's *so* hot. Oh my God, do you ever wear a kilt?"

I couldn't help myself. She was so earnestly stupid. My Gaelic was rusty and had never been great, but I leaned down and whispered, "*Is cuma sa toll feisithe liomsa.*"

The girl's eyes almost rolled back inside her tiny brain. "What does that mean?"

"You're beautiful," I lied.

Translation: *I don't give a fuck.*

An hour later, when Reagan tried to get me to go upstairs with her, I found myself totally uninterested. She'd be a fun lay, but she didn't fire my blood like another girl I'd got stuck on since the moment I first saw her. I instantly imagined wrapping that red hair around my fist, pale limbs sprawled across white sheets—

"How about we go back to the reception?" Reagan was currently trying to burrow under my jacket like an overeager monkey.

"I want to stay right here." Her quick little hands were on my belt, and I had to stop her from exposing me. Christ, I didn't need to get arrested for public indecency because some chick was desperate for cock.

I pushed her away gently, ignoring the hurt on her face.

I needed to get out of here before I did something even dumber than get married to a woman I barely knew.

Except, apparently I hadn't pushed Reagan away soon enough, because I heard an intake of breath and knew, I just fucking *knew*, who it was.

Mari. Just great.

"What's your deal?" said Reagan. The flirty woman hanging onto my arm had turned into one who looked like she'd gladly stab me in the kidney.

Couldn't blame her. I'd bolloxed this all up like a total gobshite.

"Sorry," I muttered.

I went back to the reception, but Mari wasn't there.

She's not your wife, man. Why the fuck does it matter?

It didn't matter. We weren't together. We weren't really married, as she'd told me multiple times. Yet logic wasn't on my side in this instance.

I WALKED BACK to the hotel, which was only a few blocks away. And then I was knocking on Mari's hotel room door loudly enough that I knew she'd open the door just to tell me to be quiet.

"Will you be quiet?" she said scathingly.

"You look mad, wife."

"I'm not your wife." She drew herself up. That motion put her breasts on display, and I realized she was wearing nothing but a short, silky nightgown.

How was I supposed to concentrate with her magnificent tits *right there?* Did she want me to seduce her? Based on the fact that we'd made out twice already, she wasn't immune to me. I had a feeling I could get her pussy wet and swollen within two minutes, if she didn't stab me first.

"What?" she said, breaking through my lurid thoughts. "I was sleeping."

"You left the reception twenty minutes ago. I doubt you were asleep." I moved past her into her room.

"By all means, come in. Would you like something to drink? Should I order room service, too?"

"And risk having you poison my drink? I'm good."

Mari paced behind me like an angry cat. Why hadn't I just taken her back here and fucked her until we were both drained last night? My sober brain tried to figure out the logic behind my drunken decisions, but there was no understanding it. I'd had a moment of insanity in marrying her but then not having sex with her. That was the only way to explain it.

Mari sat down on the bed, her arms crossed. She'd put on a robe that matched her nightgown. I remembered her matching emerald bra and panties last night in a heated rush. My wife liked pretty lingerie. And fuck me, but I wanted to see her wear more.

"Did you need something?" she said finally, cocking a sassy eyebrow. "Because I'm not sleeping with you."

"I was here to claim my husbandly rights, actually." I couldn't stop the brogue from dripping from my tongue. If I weren't careful, I'd end up sounding like that fucking Lucky Charms leprechaun.

"Your husbandly rights? Are you serious? Go back to your room, Liam. I'm not in the mood."

"You're jealous I was with another woman."

"Oh, you can read my mind now?"

"Nah, but you have an iron bar up your ass right now, which can't be comfortable. It's written all over your face. You're not good at hiding how you feel."

She looked so offended I had to bite back a laugh. "You don't know anything."

"What you saw at the reception…"—I shook my head —"wasn't anything. I was just messing around."

She looked away, her face in profile. I wished I had my camera right now. She'd make a beautiful model, the line of her jaw and the slim arch of her nose, her lips full and rose red. The low light in the room cast a warm glow across her pale skin. I'd have her keep the robe on, but have it sliding off one shoulder. Just a hint of sex appeal…

"I don't care who you sleep with," she said, but if I weren't studying her face, I would've missed the tremble in her bottom lip.

I felt triumph. Yeah, I felt fucking triumphant. Sue me. This woman who was so straitlaced and acted like I was a bug squashed under her shoe was jealous.

"You do care," I said. I touched her chin so she had to look me in the eyes. "You care so much that you're thinking about gouging out my eyeballs."

"I wouldn't ruin my manicure for your eyeballs."

"You'd use a spoon, then. Gloves to protect your nails. You'd figure it out."

"What a compliment."

She hadn't moved away from me, though. I wanted to flip her nightgown up, revealing what would surely be the prettiest pussy imaginable. I had a feeling it'd be as pink as her nipples. My mouth watered.

I moved my thumb down her throat, feeling her pulse flutter.

"You're jealous," I said in a low voice, "because you wanted me to fuck you. Didn't you, Mari? You can't lie to me."

She swallowed. "Physical attraction is just hormones. Chemicals. It doesn't mean anything."

"Then why are you shaking?"

"I'm cold."

"I'll warm you up."

I didn't wait for her to protest. To give me her long list of reasons, because I didn't care anymore. I didn't need to hear her pros and cons, how this wasn't in her *plan*, how it wasn't practical.

I kissed her. I kissed her like I wanted to fuck her. I licked inside her luscious mouth, and her shivers only increased.

I hauled her into my lap. I wanted her to feel how fucking hard I was for her. Her legs were splayed, and I bucked against her pelvis as I kissed her.

I wanted to blot out the memory of any man who'd kissed her before. I wanted her to forget her gobshite of an ex and only think of me.

"Is this just chemicals and hormones making you rub your pussy against me?" I said as I kissed the delicate shell of her ear.

"Liam." Her voice was a gasp.

"I know what you need." I pushed that robe off her shoulders and tossed it to the floor. I sucked on the skin of her shoulder, knowing it'd leave a mark. I ran my hand up her thigh. Her skin was silky soft, and I had to groan when she tugged at my hair.

My little wife was demanding. I wasn't complaining.

"Are you wet for me? Dripping, needing me to fill you up?" I didn't break eye contact when I pushed her panties aside, finding a soft patch of curls. I cupped her, her wetness seeping from her pussy onto my palm.

"Oh my God." She bucked and tried to find that friction, but I wasn't going to give it to her. Not yet.

She deserved to suffer for making me suffer.

"You act like you're such a good girl, but you're not. You want to be bad. Your pussy is telling me the truth about you."

Mari sighed as I parted her folds and stroked a finger from her clit to her slit, teasing her. I swiped my thumb across her aching clit. She arched and squirmed.

I palmed her ass with my other hand, realizing she was wearing a lacy thong. She was going to fucking kill me, and I wouldn't regret it one bit. "Good girls don't wear panties like these," I growled.

"That's just stereotyping," she said, her voice breathy. "I can be good and wear a thong."

I spanked her for that remark. She inhaled.

"Good girls don't wear thongs when they know their husband is coming to their room."

"I didn't know you were coming."

Her cheeks were flushed, her eyes glassy, but she sounded so defensive I laughed.

"You're full of shite, but that's fine." I thrust my index finger inside her pussy and began to rub against that spot that would drive her wild.

It took about five seconds for her eyes to start rolling back inside her head. I rubbed her clit at the same time I rubbed her g-spot. The sound of her wet pussy along with her moans and gasps had my cock aching so much I was half-afraid I'd burst inside my trousers. I hadn't done that since I'd see my first pair of bare tits in a dirty magazine as an eleven-year-old.

"You're gonna come all over my hand," I said into her neck. "Fuck yourself on my finger. You're so tight and wet."

I licked her throat as she moaned, the moan getting louder as she began to contract around my hand. Then she came with a screech that made me chuckle.

Mari, Mari, quite contrary. What was I going to do with this girl?

I petted her for a while longer as she came down from her orgasm. She'd collapsed against my chest, breathing hard. When I finally took my hand away, I caught her gaze as I licked my hand clean. She tasted tart, just like her tart, sassy mouth.

I kissed her lips, letting her taste herself. She was a languid, happy woman, and I wanted to sink inside her and fuck her so hard she'd be sore in the morning.

"That, wife, was definitely not just hormones," I whispered into her ear.

It was as if somebody lit a fire under her arse. In a rush, she scrambled from my lap, pulling her panties back in place before throwing on her robe.

"You need to leave," she bit out.

"Most women like to cuddle after I make them come. Maybe make out. I'm the big spoon, in case you were wondering."

"Please leave. I shouldn't have let you do this."

"Ah yes, I'm so cruel, making you come so hard your eyes rolled back inside your head?" I stood up and grabbed her hand, pressing it against my cock. "You really gonna leave your husband like this?"

She sniffed. "Your penis is not my problem."

"Oh, I would disagree. Entirely. Since your pussy is my problem that I already solved."

She flushed. "It was a mistake, just like last night. That's it.

Now, please leave. I have to get up early for my flight tomorrow."

I wasn't going to beg to stay. Angry and exhausted, I couldn't help but leave with one last parting shot.

"You're welcome for the orgasm, wife."

CHAPTER SEVEN

My eyes glazed over when I ended up reading the same line in this wastewater management manual for the third time. Rubbing my temples, I glanced at the clock on the wall across from my desk.

11:45. I still had five more hours of work. A workday had never moved so glacially as today.

I didn't *hate* my job. As a technical writer at a large engineering firm, I received a good salary and benefits. I had regular hours. I could take vacations; I had sick leave. We could even invest in the company's stock options, if we felt so inclined.

I'd been fortunate enough to get this job right out of college. I'd been told how lucky I was, given the economy and that I had little work experience. *Be grateful you found full-time work right away.*

I'd seen my friends and peers struggle to find jobs while I started making a cool fifty thousand a year. Not a fortune, but enough to support myself.

"Mari, have you finished editing that manual?" said my

boss, Leslie, as she stopped by my cubicle.

"Not yet. Probably by the end of the week." If I could pay attention to it long enough to edit it.

"I know you were on vacation, but we can't get behind on this project. I told Tim you'd be done today. Is there any way you could stay late to finish it tonight?"

I had at least two hundred more pages to edit. But being a good girl and not wanting to disappoint my boss, I compromised. "I can get it to you by Wednesday."

I worked until eight o'clock that night on that manual—one nobody would actually read. It was simply policy that there be a manual for every wastewater treatment plant the firm built and maintained. My job was simultaneously crucial and utterly pointless.

But what did it matter? It was a good job. Or so people liked to tell me over and over again.

Yet with each day I spent in that cubicle, editing manuals, I felt my life passing by. And now that David and I were over, I had nothing to look forward to. I couldn't use marriage and having a family to distract myself from work. From how mundane my life had become.

I think marrying a stranger is a pretty big distraction and hardly mundane, I thought wryly as I drove over to Dani's place.

Mundane? Hah. I'd tossed that out like a flaming hot potato straight through a glass window. And then the potato hit someone on the lawn, gave him a concussion, and now I was on the hook for potato-related assault.

Sometimes I still thought about becoming a makeup artist, but that job would be a huge risk. If I worked for myself, I wouldn't have benefits or stock options. There was no guarantee I'd have steady work. I could have a glut of clients and then a dearth. What if I didn't make enough during the glut to support the dearth? I'd have to come back to my old job, tail between my legs.

And now I had to consider how much money I'd drain annulling my marriage to Liam. It wouldn't be nearly as expensive as a divorce, but I could hardly consider leaving my job right now. My life was in too much limbo.

By the time I arrived at Dani's place, I briefly considered texting my sister to say I was too tired to come inside. But I needed to talk to somebody about all of this. Dani was the only one who knew—well, Dani and Jacob.

"Mari!" Dani hugged me five seconds after I entered her condo.

"Jacob isn't here," added Dani as she saw me look around. She then handed me a large glass of red wine. "He had to do flowers for a dog wedding today. Apparently it's a pug marrying a bulldog, which sounds like the ugliest puppies ever."

"People have their dog marry another dog?"

"According to the owners, they—the dogs, not the owners —met at a dog park and fell instantly in love. It was like straight out of a Hallmark movie. But probably with more humping."

Kevin, Dani's three-legged, one-eyed cat, circled around my ankles, meowing softly.

"Maybe Kevin needs a wife. Or a husband," I said.

"And cheat on me? No way." Dani picked up her cat and gave him a loud, smacking kiss, which resulted in Kevin yowling in protest.

It was then that I noticed Dani was wearing a ring on her left hand.

Dani saw where my gaze had landed, and she turned pale. "Shit. I forgot to take it off."

"Why? Are you engaged to somebody other than Jacob?" I tried to say it jokingly, but my voice was strained.

"Ha ha, no." Dani set Kevin down and ushered me into the living room. There were still boxes that had yet to be unpacked from their recent move. Kevin, for his part, began to rip up some packing paper with violent gusto.

"I wanted to tell you at a later time, but I was distracted tonight so…" Dani winced. "I'm sorry."

My sister was engaged, and she was apologizing to me. I was the worst.

"Why are you apologizing to me?" I took her hand and inspected the ring. "I'm happy for you. Why wouldn't I be? Just because my life is a dumpster fire doesn't mean yours has to be, too. Tell me everything about how he proposed."

It didn't take much to convince Dani to recount how Jacob had proposed, down to the minute detail. I'd never seen my sister positively gush before. It was almost nauseatingly heart-warming.

It was also soul-crushing, because I was selfish and terrible. My sister had found love and was getting married to her soulmate.

And my supposed soulmate? He'd cheated on me.

To compound things, I was now married to the wrong man and had to get that marriage annulled.

Clearly, marriage and I just did not get along. When had I become a walking *Friends* episode, with me being the Ross Geller of the group? Nobody wanted to be Ross.

How wrong can your latest husband be when he made you come harder than your ex ever did?

I pushed that thought aside. Just because Liam had magic, clit-rubbing fingers did not make him my knight in shining armor or my soulmate. Sex was one thing; love was another.

"Well, you can totally use all of my wedding stuff. You could even wear my dress, if you wanted," I said to Dani.

Dani gave me a weird look. "I can't do that. Besides, your dress would be way too small for me."

She was right, and I blushed, feeling foolish. I was never the one out of sorts. Dani had always been the weird sister. It was strange that I'd never consciously thought about those roles we'd always played until they'd been reversed.

I really was turning into Ross. Next I'd be yelling **WE WERE ON A BREAK!** at random people on the street.

I shrugged. "I have tons of other things—favors, center-pieces, stuff I can't even remember buying. I won't be using them."

Dani seemed incredulous. "Never? Really?"

I stared into my wineglass like it would reveal my future.

"One called-off engagement and one annulled marriage is probably enough for a girl, don't you think?"

Dani clucked her tongue. "That's dumb, and you know it. David was all wrong for you—you can't disagree with me there. Now, this Liam guy…" She slanted me a sly look. "You haven't actually told me anything about him."

"It's not like you're going to meet him."

"Still. What type of guy would cause my well-behaved older sister to throw caution to the wind? He sounds fun, at the very least."

Fun. Wicked. Sexy. Dangerous. There were a lot of words to describe my new husband. Which was why I had to get him out of my life as soon as possible.

"I threw caution to the wind because I was wasted. So wasted that getting married sounded like a great plan." I groaned. "I still can't believe I did that. How could I be so stupid? Things like this don't happen to people like me."

"Oh no, Mari is human and makes mistakes. Call the police."

I rolled my eyes. "This isn't just a mistake. It's a gargantuan situation. It's the mistake to end all mistakes. It could go in the *Guinness Book of World Records*."

"Wow. Sounds like you should get a trophy or something. It'd say something like, *Marigold Wright: First Prize for the Dumbest Mistake Ever in the History of the Universe.*"

I groaned again.

Dani laughed at me, which just made me mutter, "Why are you laughing?"

"Because what else can you do?"

"You're annoying, and I dislike you greatly."

"That's what younger sisters are for."

"How did I end up being so lucky as to have two younger sisters?"

"You're just blessed, sister dear." Dani's expression turned more serious, which made my stomach knot in anticipation. "Is it weird to admit that it's almost...nice to see you like this?"

"Nice? Seriously?"

"I mean, don't think I'm enjoying this, but for the longest time I thought..." Dani chewed on her lower lip, clearly realizing she'd already put her foot in her mouth. Being the older sister, I just cocked an eyebrow and waited for her to get herself out of this mess somehow.

"You were always so perfect when we were growing up.

You had perfect grades. You had the perfect boyfriends. You were gorgeous, tall, and smart. It seemed like you could never do anything wrong."

I stared at my sister in utter shock. I'd had no idea she'd thought of me like that.

Perfect? Me? I was holding on to my reputation by the skin of my teeth. I was flailing around like a turtle stuck on its back. There was nothing about me right now that was perfect, and I'd never been perfect. I'd worked hard to seem like I was perfect, though. The thought that my shiny exterior was losing its luster was depressing.

"But I realized within the last few months that since I'd put you on this pedestal, I didn't stop to consider how you really felt, which was shitty of me. I'm sorry."

I blew out a breath. I didn't know if I should be offended, relieved, or just confused. I was probably all three: a big, messy jumble that mirrored my life right now.

Yet I almost hated that Dani had seen through my facade. I'd always tried to put on this composed face. My life was planned, practical. I didn't do impulsive things like Dani or Kate. I was steady. I'd had to be at a young age: I'd had to keep my sisters safe when our parents had almost fallen apart.

Neither Dani nor Kate knew our parents had briefly separated when we were kids. I'd been nine, Dani seven, and Kate an infant. Our mom had told us she'd gone on a business trip, but our dad had let slip to me that our mom was unhappy and had left with only a vague explanation as to why.

I'd always remember what my dad had said to me two days after my mom had left: *She needed to find herself. She's been working too hard, with you guys, the new baby, the business. It's been too much.*

At nine, those words had translated to *you haven't been good and if you'd been good, she wouldn't have left.* I'd sit in the window of our living room, waiting for my mom to return, terrified I'd never see her again. I'd helped my dad with Dani and Kate, becoming Kate's mom for the two weeks my mom was gone. I'd tried to cook but had burned everything, because I was only nine. I'd bandaged Dani's knees when she'd fallen off her bicycle. I'd made sure Dani got on and off the school bus, or that she didn't eat too many Oreos and make herself sick. I'd changed Kate's diapers and had given her her bottle when she'd been hungry.

Then our mom had returned, and no one had said a word about the separation ever again.

I'd never told Dani and Kate because they would've been devastated knowing our mom had left because we kids had become too much to handle. So I'd shouldered the burden. I was the oldest. That was my responsibility. And it was why I preferred to keep everything in my life secure and safe and within the lines.

A man's voice broke through my reverie. "Mari, hi," said Jacob after he'd greeted Dani and kissed her. He wrapped an arm around Dani's waist. I couldn't help but notice how perfectly she fit there. "How are you?" he added.

"I'm assuming Dani has told you everything?" I said.

Jacob smiled, and if he weren't my sister's fiancé I would've swooned at his feet. He was all golden boy charm, and based on the way Dani gazed up at him, she still felt swoon-y around him.

Yet that golden boy charm did nothing to me like Liam's darker, almost sharper, handsomeness. Jacob was all charm while Liam was all masculine assertiveness. Jacob would charm your pants off with sly wit; Liam would simply rip them off before you could say yay or nay.

Jacob sat down on the oversized chair with Dani on his lap. She curled against him like a cat.

If she started purring, I was out of here. A girl could only take so much PDA from her sister.

"Pretty much everything," said Jacob, answering my question. "Dani's not exactly great at keeping secrets."

"Excuse you! I do, too," said Dani, almost squawking in protest.

"I distinctly remember you telling me Anna swore you to secrecy about her latest Tinder date, and yet you told me every single detail." Jacob grimaced. "Most of which I never needed to know."

Anna was Dani's best friend who'd she'd known since elementary school. Anna had a rather colorful dating history, even compared to my whole drunkenly-marrying-a-stranger-in-Vegas thing.

"Don't listen to him," said Dani to me, "he's just mad that I wasn't interested in having sex in a church. Which is where Anna had sex with her date, I should add."

"A church? Does she want to go to hell?" I wasn't even religious and I was about to do the sign of the cross at the mere suggestion.

"Right? Besides, pews are so uncomfortable. What happens when you bash your elbow against one? No, thanks," said Dani.

Jacob sighed. "*Anyway*. Have you contacted the lawyer I talked to?"

I blushed, because I'd been putting off going to a lawyer. I told myself it was because I'd just gotten back to Seattle, and I'd had to work, and…

Yeah, they were flimsy excuses. I was dragging my feet because I was dumb as a sack of bricks.

Orgasms have clouded your brain. Don't let a guy's ability to make you come get in the way of what's necessary. Did you forget he tried to blackmail you?

"I will," I said, "it's just been crazy lately."

Dani and Jacob exchanged a look, and I wanted to tell them this delay didn't mean anything. Yet protesting overmuch would only bring attention to the subject, so I moved the conversation back to Dani and Jacob's engagement.

By the time I got home, it was close to ten o'clock. David and I had never moved in together, mostly because it'd been easier to wait to buy a house together as a married couple. Thank God for small favors.

My apartment hadn't changed much since our breakup, except there was no longer a second toothbrush in my bathroom or the nose hair trimmer I'd gotten David for his birthday last year. Which he'd specifically asked for, I should add.

I didn't know what drew me to look at my wedding dress. Maybe it was Dani's engagement, or talking about my Vegas wedding that would soon be dissolved. Unzipping the bag, I took out the gown I should've worn a few months ago.

My heart was in my throat as I touched the chiffon skirt of my dress. An A-line gown with a lace bodice and long sleeves, it was open in the back to show a bit of skin. Classy, elegant, with a hint of sex appeal. I'd fallen in love with it the second I'd seen it in a magazine. I'd planned to wear a jeweled headband instead of a veil so the open back wouldn't be covered.

I'd thought David was the one. I'd loved him, but there hadn't been any passion. I still loved him, but with every day that passed, a smaller and smaller part of my heart remained his. If I were truly being honest, I'd fallen in love with the idea of what we'd be together more so than the man himself.

Enough reminiscing. I zipped up the bag and returned my dress to the back of my closet where it belonged.

CHAPTER EIGHT

LIAM

A week after I'd got back to Seattle, I had dinner with Niamh at our favorite sushi place in Capitol Hill. Niamh had just bought herself a car after working all summer at our uncle Henry's auto shop, and she showed the car to me like it was her new kid.

"Isn't she a beauty?" Niamh brushed a hand down the side of her Volkswagen that had to be three times older than she was. "The second I saw her, I knew she'd be mine."

"Did you help fix her up?"

"Duh. Put in a new transmission, brakes, everything. I wouldn't let anyone touch her, except for when Uncle Henry got mad at me for messing with the engine. He said I didn't know what I was doing and could've gotten hurt."

I wished Niamh were less like me, but Christ Almighty she was just as stubborn and impulsive. As a toddler, I had to buy a leash to keep her from running into traffic. I'd got a reputation in town for being the teenager who took his sister out for walks like a dog.

As the years passed, Niamh hadn't lost that willfulness. She did whatever she wanted and apologized later. That included: cutting off all her hair in sixth grade; climbing up the highest tree back in Ireland and getting stuck when she was seven; eating a caterpillar because a boy dared her when she was twelve; and a few months ago, she'd bleached her black hair and dyed it blue. Aunt Siobhan had called me and yelled into the phone about my sister for an hour that particular evening.

She's going to be the death of me! She never listens to me or Henry. Can you talk some sense into her?

No, I couldn't, and I wouldn't be the one to extinguish my sister's spark. She was a handful, but that made her interesting. The last thing I wanted was for my sister to become less than she was.

One thing I hoped she never discovered? Boys. She was still too much of a tomboy, thank God. The first guy who looked at my sister sideways would see the side of my fist.

She reminded me of another obnoxiously stubborn woman, actually.

I pushed thoughts of Mari aside when Niamh and I went inside the sushi place to eat. Although it was a Wednesday, it was packed with scarf-wearing hipsters. Niamh's blue hair didn't stand out here.

"How was the wedding?" Niamh asked after we'd ordered a plate of sashimi and sushi to share. Niamh propped her chin in her hands, her blue hair complementing her blue eyes.

With creamy skin, naturally dark hair, and a sharp tongue, she reminded me so much of Mam that it hurt sometimes. Niamh didn't remember Mam much since she'd died when Niamh was only four. Niamh didn't even have a tinge of Irish brogue to her speech, having lived in the States since she was six. At the time, I'd got a gig over in Washington from one of

Uncle Henry's friends, and we'd both immigrated here. It had helped that Mam had been a dual US-Irish citizen, so both Niamh and I were able to become dual citizens as well.

The wedding. *Which one?* I thought darkly. My friends' or my own that I'd done when I'd been so rat-arsed I'd thought it had been a great fucking idea?

I hadn't seen Mari since we'd got back to Seattle. I hadn't had time to talk to a lawyer yet, although I had a feeling Mari hadn't wasted any time on that front. That shouldn't have rankled. I didn't *know* her. We weren't really married.

But it hurt that she was so determined to get rid of me, her dirty little secret.

"The wedding was fine," I said finally.

"Poor Liam, forced to act like he was happy for his friend getting married."

"I *am* happy for Sam."

"You look thrilled."

Niamh mimicked my expression—brooding and sullen—that I couldn't help but laugh.

"The wedding *was* fine. People got married and drank too much. Now, tell me about your college applications. When do you hear back from each school?"

Niamh's sullen expression instantly transformed to an excited one. She began to list all of the Ivy League schools she was applying to—Harvard, Yale, Brown, Stanford—telling me all about the recommendation letters she'd asked from her teachers and tennis coach.

"Asked them? You mean you wrote them and they signed them," I said before popping a sushi roll into my mouth.

Niamh wrinkled her nose. "I might have given *suggestions.*"

"Sure, just like you *suggested* that Aunt Siobhan's car should get a new paint job, and you painted it pink for her. She sure loved that idea."

"That was forever ago!"

"You haven't changed." I pointed to her bare plate. "Eat. You're too skinny."

"You sound like some old Irish grandma."

But Niamh started eating and talking. I could just imagine Aunt Siobhan telling her to chew with her mouth closed. *Be ladylike, Niamh!* But I didn't give a shit if my sister wasn't ladylike. She was smart and ambitious, and she'd get to go to her dream college.

"What's your safety school?" I said. "University of Washington?"

Niamh squirmed in the booth. "Um—"

"Don't tell me you didn't apply to a safety school."

"I don't want to go to U-dub!"

I sighed. "It's a perfectly good school."

"I know, I know." Niamh chewed on her bottom lip. "But I don't want to stay here. You get it. You've never lived anywhere long. And U-dub just doesn't have the political science departments like the Ivies do."

"But what if you don't get into any of them? Are you just not going to college in the fall?" I hated even suggesting it, but it had to be said. My sister wasn't great about considering the pitfalls of her decisions.

She lifted her chin, the stubborn brat. "That won't happen. There's no way I won't get into at least one of them."

I hoped she was right. I didn't want to see how devastated she'd be if she didn't get even one acceptance.

After we'd finished eating, I walked Niamh to her car and told her to behave herself.

"Don't stick your hands into any more engines," I said. "I don't need another phone call from Aunt Siobhan about how you're driving her insane."

"Aw, Liam. Don't be like that." Niamh threw her arms around my neck and hugged me.

I sighed inwardly. She wasn't a toddler on a leash anymore, but I almost wished she were. She was easier to control at that age. Now I could only advise and help her up when she stumbled.

"Be good," I said, trying to sound firm.

"*Mo ghrá thu*," she said with a bright smile before she drove off. *I love you.* It was one of the few phrases Niamh remembered in Gaelic.

Before we'd moved to the States, I'd worked odd jobs while raising Niamh on my own. She'd been so young that it hadn't taken long before she'd mostly forgotten that she'd had a mam at all. I became her parents, wrapped up in a too-young package.

She'd never known Da. He'd walked out on us when Mam had been pregnant with her.

I could've let Niamh be raised in foster care. No one would've blamed me. What the hell did I know about raising a child, only eighteen years old? When Mam had got sick and passed, I hadn't even known how to cook or do laundry. But Mam had made me promise to take care of my little sister. I wasn't about to break that promise—not then, and not now.

I thought of when Niamh had started primary school, and she'd clung to my leg that first day. Her teacher, a Mrs. O'Shaughnessy, had been a jolly, kind woman who'd worked with young children for so many years that nothing fazed her.

"Come on, dear, it's your first day of school," said Mrs. O'Shaughnessy, kneeling in front of Niamh.

Niamh clung more tightly to me, her little fingers surprisingly strong. I had to get to work, and I impatiently detached her fingers from my trousers.

"I have to go," I said, even as she started crying.

"Nooooooooo," she wailed. She threw herself onto my feet.

At that age, Niamh had a tendency to be melodramatic. If I wanted her to eat peas, she'd throw herself on the ground. If I wanted her to brush her hair, she'd act like I'd wanted to set her hair on fire.

So it didn't occur to me that Niamh would take my leaving her at school that day as me abandoning her. When I came to get her that afternoon, Mrs. O'Shaughnessy told me Niamh had cried the entire day. She'd only been soothed when they'd eaten lunch—nothing could distract my sister like a good pudding.

Niamh was extra clingy for weeks after that. Dropping her off at school became a more complicated affair. It reached a breaking point when Mrs. O'Shaughnessy called me while I was at work to ask that I come pick her up because she was disrupting the class.

We walked home in silence. I was frustrated and even more frustrated that I was losing money while taking this time off from work. When we reached home, though, Niamh sat down in the middle of our tiny flat and wouldn't talk the rest of the afternoon and into the evening.

It took until I put her to bed for her to ask me, "Are you going to leave again?"

"Leave? I'm not going anywhere."

"Like Mam left. She isn't here anymore, and you might not come back, too."

The guilt I felt was overwhelming. I hadn't realized Niamh had thought that every day I'd taken her to school that it might be the last time she'd see me. I'd thought she was too young to remember Mam's passing.

After that, I always assured my sister I would never leave her. Even when she started living with our aunt and uncle, I'd vowed I would never be more than a phone call away from her.

I pushed the memories aside when I arrived back at my flat. I needed to work on editing the photos I'd taken a week ago. It wasn't a paying gig—just an impromptu trip into the mountains for some much-needed time alone. Mount Rainier featured in most of the photos, white-tipped with snow. There had been more and more snowfall the further I'd hiked. It had reminded me of winters in Ireland, except this time I hadn't had to hoard my food to make sure Niamh had enough to eat.

My eyes felt like they had pebbles in them after staring at Photoshop for two hours. Yawning, I closed my laptop and began to open the mail I'd neglected since I'd gone to Vegas.

When I opened the envelope without a return address, I should've known it wouldn't be anything good.

In strained handwriting, my grandda—or old man Gallagher, as I thought of him—wrote to remind me that Niamh would receive her inheritance as long as we both "took care to keep within the bounds of propriety." I scowled as I read the letter until I wished I had a fireplace to burn it in. That arsehole. What year did he think it was?

A chill ran up my spine a moment later.

Mari. My drunken marriage. The annulment.

Jesus Christ, if old man Gallagher found out about this he'd disinherit Niamh. He was petty enough to do it. The fact that he hadn't yet was a fucking miracle.

Old man Gallagher had hated Mam because he'd thought she wasn't good enough for his son. Da had married Mam without his own da's consent, and apparently it had rocked the entire island. Or so Mam had always told me. *Your grandda nearly blew his brains out,* she'd say with amusement.

I'd thought that old man Gallagher would help me and Niamh after Da had run off and Mam had died. I'd called; I'd written him letters. I'd borrowed my friend's car and drove up to his place, but I'd been turned away without a single explanation.

I'd done my level best to take care of my sister on my own. My worst fear had been that she'd be taken away from me.

Old man Gallagher had terrified me when I'd been a kid. He'd been the type of person to put you in your place with a single look. Once when he'd asked me how my marks were in school, I'd pretty much pissed myself when he'd pronounced I'd get nowhere with those kinds of grades.

I'd been five years old.

A year after Mam had died, old man Gallagher sent me and Niamh letters to inform us that he'd included us in his will. I'd been tempted to tell the old man to go to hell. Why would he write us into his will now when he'd not cared if we'd starved on the streets for a year? But I'd given in because Niamh was getting the bulk of the money anyway.

Nice guy, my grandda.

I'd already got my inheritance a decade ago since I was older than eighteen. I'd spent the money on photography equipment and the best whiskey I could get my hands on in podunk Georgia.

At that point, Niamh had already been living with our aunt Siobhan and uncle Henry—Mam's sister and her husband—and I'd been wandering around the States like a stray dog, taking photos, sleeping with women, and getting into fights at bars when I had too much to drink.

I knew deep in my bones that old man Gallagher was spiteful enough to disinherit my sister because of my mistake with Mari, though. And then Niamh's chance of attending an Ivy League would go up in smoke. I couldn't afford to pay for Ivy League tuition. She deserved the best life I could give her. She was too fucking brilliant to go to a state school, no matter what I said to her about safety schools. She would get to do something amazing with her life—unlike me.

Niamh only had six more months before she turned eighteen and she'd get her inheritance. The thought that I'd destroyed my baby sister's chances to make the best of her life made me want to vomit. I couldn't let my drunken mistake ruin Niamh's life.

"I have to stay married to Mari." Saying the words out loud made them real—and fucking terrifying.

I broke open the bottle of whiskey I used for special occasions—yes, I was a walking Irish cliché, fucking sue me—because I had no idea how I'd get Mari to agree.

Like it'd be that much of a burden.

Fine, I was attracted to my wife. I wanted her in my bed. I wasn't dead, and she was a gorgeous, alluring spitfire of a woman.

I thought of how she'd felt as her pussy clenched around my finger. The look of surprise on her face when her orgasm had rolled through her. How she'd tasted on my fingers, how she'd kissed me back with a ferocity that had surprised even cynical ol' me.

It wouldn't exactly be a hardship to stay married to her.

I had some money. Not enough for Niamh's tuition, but enough that I could bribe Mari to agree to this scheme.

Even prim little women like Mari Wright could be bought for the right price.

I smiled darkly into my whiskey. Mari thought she was done with me?

No chance in hell.

CHAPTER NINE

MARI

'I have a proposition for you," said Liam without preamble.

When Liam had texted me a week after we'd returned from Las Vegas to ask that we meet in a neutral place, I hadn't hesitated.

Now I wondered why I *hadn't* hesitated. Apparently him giving me an amazing orgasm had fried my brain and made me forget he was a giant jerk-wad.

"A proposition," I repeated. "Why do I not want to know what that means?"

His grin was too easy, his body language almost languid. Like he knew I'd agree before I'd said the magic *yes* word. It was annoying.

We'd decided to meet in a neutral place, a coffee shop in Ballard that currently had an array of customers, including a man with a blue macaw on his shoulder. No one batted an eye at the bird even when it squawked random words at other customers. *Beans! Coffee! Llamas!*

Last week in Ballard, I'd seen a guy wearing a cat in a front pack so random pets were pretty normal around here.

"I don't need people knowing we got married when we were drunk in Vegas," Liam continued, stretching his long legs out in front of him, "but I can't agree to an annulment, either."

I stared at him in shock. "You *can't agree?* I don't understand. You don't want to stay married to me. Don't you hate marriage?"

"You underestimate your charms."

I rolled my eyes. "Flattery will get you nowhere."

"You didn't say that that night in your hotel room."

I kicked him under the table. His smile just broadened, the jerk.

"Can I tell you, or are you just going to assault me?" he said, smooth as butter.

"Wait, let me guess." I tapped my chin, thinking. "Do you need an heir for your glorious Irish estate? Because you're actually an Irish lord?" I covered my mouth, faking a gasp. "Does that mean I'm a duchess?"

"If I were a lord, I wouldn't be having this discussion with you. Besides, there are only two Irish dukedoms total. The likelihood I'd have one is slim to none."

"Too bad." I clucked my tongue. "I would've liked being called 'my lady.'"

"'Your grace.'" When I raised an eyebrow, Liam shrugged. "My sister made me watch *Downton Abbey* with her. Branson deserved better, by the way."

Despite the lighthearted banter, my heart was pounding like a drum. Stay married? What would my family and friends say? One second I was engaged to David, then we were calling off our wedding, and then I was married to *another* man? The whispers and questions alone would be terrible.

Liam leaned toward me, his languidness dissolving in an instant. "Look, I have something on the line that'll be fucked if word gets out I married you and then got an annulment, proving to everyone that it was a huge mistake."

I reared back. "You think I don't have anything on the line? This isn't something I want people to know about, either."

Liam smirked, but there was a flash of something in his eyes I didn't recognize. "Don't want people knowing about your dirty little secret?"

"No, I don't want people to know I drunkenly married a stranger in Vegas. Is that so crazy? And it isn't the *who* in this instance; it's the marriage in general. I'd be saying the same thing to any other man I'd randomly married after drinking too much tequila."

"Make it a habit? Marrying strange men?"

I flushed. "No. You're my first."

"I'm happy to hear it."

He imbued the words with innuendo, and I squirmed in my seat. Memories of that night in the hotel room flashed in my mind. Right then, I could practically feel his hands on my body, the way I begged him to touch me—

I hardened my heart and my voice. "I'm not staying married to a man I wouldn't have chosen if I hadn't been drunk. Period."

If Liam was offended, he masked it quickly.

"I'm not proposing we stay married forever. I don't want that, either."

"Then what *do* you want?"

He sighed, ruffling his dark hair. He hadn't shaved this morning, and it made him seem more rugged than usual. I couldn't help but remember how that scruff had felt as he'd kissed me.

"I have a sister," he said finally. "She's a lot younger than me. I basically raised her myself. She's turning eighteen in six months, and she'll get a large inheritance from our grandda when she's of age. She'll use it to go to college."

"That sounds like something out of *Downton Abbey*. Are you sure you're not a duke?"

"Very."

"So what does our marriage have to do with your sister's inheritance?"

Liam sighed. "Our grandda is a nutter. If he finds out about this, he'll disinherit Niamh. And it'll have been my fault."

I almost laughed, because it sounded *so* absurd. This had to be some kind of elaborate prank, right?

But Liam wasn't laughing. I chewed on the inside of my cheek.

I said, "How would he even find out? Is he in the US?"

"No, but he'd find out. He always does, believe me. He's a wily old shite. And any paperwork associated with an annulment is a matter of public record. I looked into it. It can't be sealed."

"Why would your grandfather punish your sister because of you?"

"He's always hated us." Liam folded his hands. "Look, you don't need to know my sordid family history. Just that I need you to go along with this. I can pay you for your trouble. And as a guarantee, we'll divorce, and I won't fight you if you want spousal support. An annulment wouldn't give you that."

My mouth was dry. Money—money I could use to quit my

job. I could pursue my dream of becoming a makeup artist instead of wasting my life in a job I hated more and more every day.

If Liam had said this inheritance was for him, I would've told him tough luck. But I understood wanting to protect younger sisters. I knew it like I knew my own face in the mirror. It was something older siblings took on without even realizing it the moment our younger siblings were born.

"My sister Niamh is brilliant," said Liam to fill the silence. "She can go to any university she wants. She's only applying to Ivies, for Christ's sake. She has a 4.2 GPA and will be her school's valedictorian of a class of seven hundred."

Was Liam, who was normally so confident bordering on arrogant, almost on his knees, begging me to agree to this? To my surprise, I felt almost jealous of his sister. What would it be like to have that kind of devotion from a man like him?

Liam continued, "If you agree to this, we'd have to act like we're really married. Live together and everything."

"Yeah, like that'll be so easy. Where are we going to live?"

"My flat."

"Why not mine?"

"Does yours have a second bedroom?"

He had me there. "No. It's a small one bedroom." And annoyingly enough, my lease was up soon and I hadn't signed another one yet.

Life was so convenient when you didn't need it to be.

"Say yes, Mari." Liam took my hands, his gaze entreating. "Just six months. Then you'll get your money, Niamh will get hers, and it'll be like none of this ever happened."

The fact that I wasn't saying no right away scared me. I must be insane. I needed to get my brain examined. If I had an MRI done, they'd most likely point to a part of my brain and diagnose me with Liam Gallagher Syndrome. *It's curable, but only if you run far, far away from the virus himself.*

"Wait, if we're living together…" I lowered my voice. "Are you suggesting we sleep together, too?" If I said the words too loudly, I'd probably summon a demon. Or Liam's magnificent cock. Both were equally dangerous.

"I wouldn't say no." Liam crossed his arms, smiling.

"Uh, I would!"

My palms were sweating. If I slept with Liam, I'd act even more stupidly than I was right now. I'd probably be dumb enough to fall in love with him. A girl had to know her limits. Liam using the full force of his charm along with the full force of his cock would break more than my lady parts.

"We'll live as chastely as nuns," he said. He leaned forward, whispering like I had been earlier. "You know you want to say yes. Six months, Mari. And by the end, you'll be the one richer."

"I'll think about it," was all I could manage.

He was still holding my hands. I was about to pull away, but then he brought my hand to his mouth and kissed the back of it.

"Your grace," he said gravely.

Oh, he was dangerous. So very, very dangerous—to my lady bits and to my heart.

"No sex," I said firmly. "If I agree to this, we're going to act like both of us are totally incapable of intercourse."

Liam's lips twitched. "Not sure my dick will agree to that stipulation."

"It'll have to. It's not getting anything from me."

"So you're saying you didn't enjoy how I made you come so hard you left marks on my shoulders?"

I was so red I was probably on fire. "Will you keep your voice down?"

"I'm not ashamed. Why should you be?"

Wings flapping overhead snagged my attention. The blue macaw settled a foot from where Liam sat, its long talons curling over the wooden edge of the booth. One of its beady eyes stared at Liam before swiveling toward me. I was pretty sure it could see right through me. It was unnerving.

"Cookie Monster, come back here," said the bird's owner. "You're a very bad boy."

Cookie Monster ruffled its feathers and then proceeded to fly onto a shelf that probably once held a speaker but was currently empty. It was also all the way up to the ceiling, at least eight-feet high.

"Cookie Monster! No! Get back down here!" said the owner.

"Maybe you should give him some cookies as a bribe," drawled Liam.

I kicked him under the table. I did not want that bird coming back down to stare at me and suss out all my deep dark secrets.

But it didn't matter. Because Cookie Monster decided to ruffle its feathers again and then squawk in the loudest possible bird voice, "MADE YOU COME SO HARD."

"Made you come, made you come," it repeated as it hopped from one end of the shelf to the other. "Made you COOOOOOOME!"

"Oh my God," I said as I buried my face in my hands. Liam, the jerk, was laughing silently.

Cookie Monster's owner spluttered and rifled through his oversized man-purse for a plastic bag. "Look, a cookie! Just for you!"

"MADE YOU COME SO HARD," was the bird's screeching response.

Around us, people were laughing or looking like they'd prefer a coffee shop with less pornographic entertainment. I was one of them.

Liam was still laughing, and even though I wanted to melt into the floor, I couldn't resist laughing, either.

"This isn't funny," I said, even as I tried to keep a straight face.

"Sir, you need to get your bird," said one of the baristas in a harried voice.

"MADE YOU COME!"

"Sir, *now.*"

The owner waved one of the cookies in the air, and finally the evil bird flew down to retrieve its bribe. It settled on its owner's shoulder and proceeded to scatter bird-cookie crumbs all over the floor.

After pretty much pulling Liam from the cafe, I hoped he'd forget about the whole sex-ban thing. But it was as if my luck had totally run out lately. If it wasn't an X-rated bird, it was my husband not letting something go. Whose dog had I run over to cause this epic karmic punishment?

"So you're saying yes?" asked Liam as he walked me to my car.

"It's a maybe right now."

"I'm gonna need an answer soon."

I swallowed and asked the question I'd been afraid to utter. "What happens if I say no? What will you do?"

"Nothing."

I stared at him in shock. "Really. Nothing? Didn't you try to blackmail me at the wedding to keep this thing silent?"

Liam shrugged. "I was bluffing. I wouldn't need to blackmail you, now that I know you. Because you'd always feel guilty that you caused a young girl to lose everything. Because you understand what it's like to protect your sisters."

Oh, I hated him right then. I hated that he'd already figured me out. I hated that he'd use my own conscience against me.

His sister wasn't my problem. It wouldn't be my fault if this grandfather of theirs decided to be spiteful.

It wouldn't be my fault, technically, but I was good at taking on guilt that hadn't been labeled as mine. I'd done it for a time after I'd discovered David had cheated on me. I'd done it when my mom had left for those long two weeks years ago. I'd done it when I'd considered leaving my boss high and dry to pursue my true passion.

I hated Liam, because he saw straight through me to my messy, shadowed center.

"You're evil," I said. It was a lame response, but it was all I could manage.

He looked almost sad. "I know."

"Six months. That's it. Then we're getting a divorce and I get my money."

"I'll draft up a contract. A real one."

"And I'm sleeping in my own room."

He nodded.

"What will we tell everyone?" I whispered.

"We'll figure that out together."

I put out my hand. "Then you have a deal, husband."

CHAPTER TEN

LIAM

A week after Mari and I signed our contract, and three days after Mari moved into my place, I cursed myself for being the greatest fool alive.

Live together, I'd said, *it'll be fine,* I'd said.

Except it wasn't fucking fine. Mari was in my space, her smell, her voice, her very being taking up both my physical and mental space.

She'd filled my fridge with chick food. I was pretty sure she'd bought at least one bottle of rosé and one bottle of chardonnay, both of which I never allowed near my kitchen for obvious reasons. She'd filled my bathroom cabinets with so many items—how did women have so much *stuff?*

It had been so long since I'd lived with a woman I'd forgotten they collected products like magpies collected things for their nests. They had soap for each body part. They had tweezers and clippers and tiny scissors; they had lotion and razors and hair spray. And so much makeup. Thankfully Mari had kept most of her makeup in her bedroom—my second bedroom—because there wasn't room for it in my tiny-ass bathroom.

But the tampons under the sink, the nail polish left on the coffee table? That was one thing.

Having Mari *here*, underfoot? It was the worst sort of torture. Because she'd told me she didn't want me to touch her again, and I wanted to break that promise so badly. My cock was in a perpetual state of arousal. Mari would push her hair over her shoulder, and it would get excited. I was going to have to shove an icepack down my trousers for six months if I didn't get my head on straight.

It's for Niamh, I reminded myself. *You're not a fucking pussy, Gallagher. Suck it up. She's your roommate who also happens to be your wife. You've gone through worse.*

On Friday, Mari got up early to go to work. I heard her turn on the shower, which was torture, imagining her wet and naked. I heard her make herself a smoothie. Torture, because the blender was fucking loud at seven AM. I heard her blow-dry her hair, which was also way too loud.

"Mari," I said gruffly after she'd shut off the blow-dryer. "Can you do that at night?"

She blinked in surprise. "What? Dry my hair?"

"Yeah. It's way too loud." I yawned.

Her lips twitched. "I guess you're not a morning person?"

"No. And I work for myself, so I get up when I want."

"You could buy some earplugs."

"I don't like those things."

"Poor baby." She wrinkled her pert little nose. "I'll try not to wake you up again, but I make no promises. You might just have to get up earlier. Because you were the one who came up with this scheme, dear husband."

I scowled and stalked to the kitchen to put on a pot of coffee. I wasn't going back to sleep now. I might as well get some work done.

Mari had settled in without much issue, I'd give her that. She'd taken over my flat, just like if she were my real wife. I had a feeling she was doing it as a bit of revenge for making her move in with me, as opposed to me moving into her place.

Mari left for work a few minutes later. When she opened the front door, she said, "See you tonight," but then blushed, stuttered something, and shut the door in a hurry.

Something inside my chest twisted. *See you tonight.* Such a normal, wifely thing to say.

My brain wanted to fall down the "what would it be like if Mari was really my wife" rabbit hole. Would she sleep in late with me on the weekends? Would she kiss me goodbye, tell me she'd miss me while she was at work? Would she let me fuck her on every available surface in my flat like a good, obedient wife should?

For the love of Christ, stop.

But I couldn't let myself fall down that rabbit hole. That was for stupid girls like Alice who thought running after rabbits was totally logical.

I forced my thoughts on my work. At the moment, I was editing photos I'd taken for a newly opened building at the University of Washington. Not the most exciting job, but it paid well.

My interest in photography had started when I'd got a disposable camera at a friend's wedding when I was kid. Mam had had an old Polaroid I could play with, but it took crappy photos. The disposable camera wasn't much better, but at least the photos weren't all sepia-toned. I'd gone out to the fields near our house, trying to be artistic as I took photos of cows, trees, and a random fire hydrant.

I'd been so excited when I'd got the photos developed. I'd saved up the money to get it done at the local drugstore. But they'd been mostly blurry, or I'd taken a photo of the cow's arse when I'd tried to get the entire cow in the photo.

Photography kept me going through the good times and bad. I got better and better at it. And when I'd had to drop out of school to take care of Niamh, I'd had enough skill to get work.

After editing those UW photos, I went for a walk to clear my head. As I walked, I took some photos of people in a nearby park: moms wrapped up in coats, pushing babies in strollers; young kids playing on the playground; an old man feeding pigeons.

By the time I returned to my flat, Mari had come back from work and was cooking in the kitchen.

"Liam!" she called out, "where's your colander?"

"The fuck is a colander?" I came into the kitchen to see various pots and pans on the stove. One had something red in it, the other something green.

"You know, to drain pasta?" Mari let out a long-suffering sigh. "I threw mine out because it was old. I thought you'd have one…"

"Darling, I don't cook. I order takeout or use the microwave."

She scrunched up her nose. "You're such a cliché."

"Good thing I have a sweet wife to make me dinner every night."

"This isn't for you."

I dipped my finger into the red stuff, which was a rather tasty marinara.

"You sure are making a lot for just one person. This is good. This might not be a terrible bargain after all, with you cooking for me."

She raised the wooden spoon she was holding and pointed it at me. "I am *not* your personal chef, Liam Gallagher. I am cooking for myself like I do most nights. If you happen to eat some of this food, that is your choice. But I'm not catering any of it to your tastes."

"Good thing I enjoy your tastes."

Mari flushed, clearly annoyed. She reached for the boiling pot on the back of the stove, only to let out a yelp when she tried to pick up the metal handle.

"Ow, crap—"

"Come here." I took her by the wrist to the kitchen sink.

"Wait, the pasta—"

I flicked off the burner, set the pot on a towel sitting on the counter, and then turned on the sink. A red splotch covered Mari's palm.

"You have to be careful," I said as I ran warm water over the burn.

"Shouldn't it be cold water?" She winced.

"Warm is better. Keep your hand under the water. I'll be right back."

After digging around under my bathroom sink, which was way too full of Mari's stuff now, I found the aloe vera I'd bought when I'd stupidly gone to the lake without wearing sunscreen, plus some gauze from when I'd cut my hand on a piece of metal while working at a skate park years ago.

"I can't believe I forgot to use an oven mitt," said Mari sheepishly. "I'm usually not stupid enough to grab a hot metal pot handle."

I poured some aloe vera on her palm. "It doesn't look too bad. Hopefully it won't blister."

I wrapped her hand in the gauze before taping it off. For reasons I didn't want to think about, I was reluctant to let go of her hand. She'd painted her fingernails a pale pink, the tips white. I couldn't help but notice that there was a lighter strip of skin on her left ring finger.

"I need to get you a ring," I said.

Mari pulled her hand back. "Oh, no. Don't spend the money."

She was right, of course. There was no reason to buy a ring for a fake marriage. But the fact that she still had her ex's mark on her finger in a way sent me into a jealous tailspin. I wanted her to wear *my* ring.

"Don't worry about it. You need one if anyone is going to believe our story. I'll need one, too."

"Oh, well. I guess that makes sense. The ring pop I got at our wedding won't really work."

The heat of the kitchen had curled the baby hairs around her forehead and against her neck. This close, I could see a smattering of freckles on her nose that would darken in the summer.

Her lips were rosebud pink, her eyes a sea green. They seemed greener today, and I realized she'd used purple-toned eyeshadow, which was a clever trick. She'd also dusted something shimmery on her cheeks. And when I peered more closely, it seemed like she'd used something darker along the edges of her face and jaw.

I touched her chin to turn her face toward me, stopping her from plating the food.

"Your face looks different," I said. I turned her toward the light. "What did you do?"

"That's not really a great compliment to give a woman."

"Tell me."

"Do you really want a makeup lesson right now?"

I'd never paid any attention to women's makeup before, except when necessary for photos. The wrong type of makeup could make a huge difference in how photos turned out. Otherwise, though, it was one of those things that didn't enter into my brain space.

But right now I didn't want a damn lesson. I wanted to keep touching her. I wanted to feel the silkiness of her skin against my fingers. I wanted to make her pant my name like she had in the hotel room in Vegas.

I traced the line of her jaw. "Tell me," I repeated.

She swallowed visibly, especially when I caressed the shell of her ear.

"Um, well, it's called contouring. You use shadows and highlights to accentuate your features."

I touched the bridge of her nose. "You have some here." I skipped my fingers up to her temples. "Also here."

"It's kind of like painting."

"Or editing a photo."

She let out a small laugh. "Pretty much the same principles, yeah."

My cock was hard, painfully so, and when Mari licked her bottom lip, I was five seconds away from tossing her over my shoulder.

But Mari was skittish. I'd learned that much about her. If I wanted to get my hands in her panties a second time, I couldn't push her too hard too fast. Even if my cock wanted to do everything hard and fast.

I gently pulled her hair from its ponytail. Lifting a section of it to my nose, I inhaled before wrapping it around my fingers.

"If you don't want me to kiss you," I said, "then you should tell me now."

"Would you let me go if I said I didn't want you to?"

"Yes. But only after doing my best to persuade you to change your mind."

My other hand drifted down her back and settled right above the cleft of her arse.

"I'm not sure that counts as really asking for someone's consent," she whispered.

I should let her go. This was going to complicate everything. Although considering we were already married after a stupid drunken night in Vegas, we'd basically created a brand-new definition of *complicated*. That Facebook status wouldn't contain how complicated this entire shit-show was.

"Tell me to leave you alone," I said.

Tell me to go. Tell me to never touch you again. Because I don't think I have the strength not to.

She didn't say anything for a long moment. I could see thoughts flit across her face. She was as conflicted as I felt, which meant that I could get her to say yes without much persuasion.

I caressed her cheek. "Five, four, three," I started counting down. "Two—"

"No, I don't want you to leave me alone," she admitted finally.

Triumph raced through me. I kissed her, groaning into her mouth. She tasted like cherries and summertime. I licked inside her mouth, wishing I could kiss her in other places—her breasts, her belly; her pussy, the cleft of her ass. I'd even suck on her toes if she'd let me, I was that far gone, and I wasn't exactly into feet. But Mari had pretty feet; she had pretty everything. It was intoxicating.

"Your beard," she whispered when I sucked on the side of her neck. "It's scratchy."

"I'll shave it."

"No—I mean, I like it." I could see her swallow.

It was my turn to groan. The thought of her throat, her chin, all marked from my beard sent me into a tailspin of desire. I wanted to set her on top of the counter and fuck her until this madness was purged from me. Surely once would be enough. It always was. Every woman I'd ever been with had bored me eventually.

My wife would become one of those women. She had to, because she was leaving me in six months with her money and never looking back.

I rubbed my cock against her pelvis. "Do you know how often I jerk off thinking of you?" I growled, almost angry. "How I think about how your pussy clenched around my fingers that night in Vegas?"

She shuddered. "You think about me?"

Jesus, how could she not know? "You're like some kind of virus."

She let out a strained laugh. "I'm sorry? Maybe you

should see somebody about that. If there's a burning sensation, it's probably chlamydia."

I looked up into her smiling face. I smacked her arse for that remark, and she yelped.

"My dick is clean, you little brat."

"You're the one accusing me of infecting you."

"You have. That's the only explanation. Or you're a witch." I chuckled. "Actually, I know what you are: a *leanan sídhe.*"

"What in the world is that? And how do you say that again?"

I repeated the words slowly, *lee-a-nan sithe.* Mari repeated them back with a charmingly terrible accent.

"Is that some kind of Gaelic creature?" she then asked.

"Kind of." I licked a path down her throat to her collarbone. "It's a beautiful woman who comes to artists and becomes their lover. In return for divine inspiration, she basically sucks the life out of them. They die young, but they create lasting art and have amazing sex so it's a fair trade."

"First I'm a virus, now I'm a vampire? How has any woman slept with you? You're terrible at compliments."

"Wasn't a compliment. Just a statement of fact."

She sighed. Soon I was kissing her again, not caring if she did, in fact, suck out my life force as payment. My cock wasn't exactly the most discerning when it came to life and death situations.

We kissed for so long that it was only when the smoke detector started screaming that we realized the marinara sauce had dried up and had started burning.

"Shit," I said, grabbing a towel to wave at the smoke detector. "Will you shut the fuck up?"

The alarm squealed a bit longer, as if saying to me, *you're the dumbass who left the sauce on the burner for way too long.*

Mari moaned as she tried to stir what was left. "So much for dinner."

When I tried to kiss her temple, though, she ducked her head. "I think you've made your point."

"My point?"

She was still stirring that damn sauce, like if she did it long enough it'd come back to life.

"I'm attracted to you. I won't disagree there. But that doesn't mean we need to keep doing this."

"Why the fuck not?"

"This is temporary." She said the words slowly, and it only pissed me off more. "And I can't just have sex and not have my feelings be involved."

"Whoever said anything about feelings? This is about feeling good. Physical only. And we're stuck together. Why not work off some steam while we're at it?"

She flicked a glance over her shoulder at me. "I'm a commitment kind of girl. You already know that. You said yourself that you don't do commitment. So I'd rather take you at your word. 'When people tell you who they are, believe them.'"

She was using my own words against me. I wanted to tell her that—what? I was going to be a real husband? That I didn't want this marriage to end?

No, I wanted it to end. Marriage was pointless; love was just a fairy tale. If it did exist, it disappeared under the strain of reality.

"You know what? I don't need this. I can get any woman I want. I don't have to beg."

"Congratulations," was Mari's deadpan reply.

"But if you think you can resist me for six months, you're wrong." I wrapped an arm around her waist and kissed the side of her neck, loving that she shuddered when my lips touched her skin. "You're not immune to me, wife. Remember that."

CHAPTER ELEVEN

MARI

That Saturday, I found myself hiding in my parents' bathroom during a family dinner. Why? Oh, I'd just told everyone I was married now and living with my husband. Surprise!

At the moment, I was avoiding speaking to my husband. Because I knew that if I spoke to him, he'd try something. Like seduce me.

So I kept our conversations as unsexy as possible if I needed to say anything at all. A guy can't really work with questions like "Where's the toilet paper?" and "When does your recycling go out?" Not even someone like Liam Gallagher, seduction expert.

But now I had a more important issue than the possibility of making recycling bins sexy: explaining to my family that I was married.

The conversation thus far before I'd run to hide in the bathroom had been as follows:

"You're *what?*"

"To who? David? Did he beg for you to take him back?"

"Why would you marry David? He cheated on you. He sucks."

"Are you joking? You have to be joking. It's not a good joke, Mari. Stop this."

My parents and my youngest sister, Kate, had lobbed questions at me like tomatoes at a bad actor in a play. Dani and Jacob, who already knew all about this, had remained silent. Dani had shot me concerned looks every few seconds, though.

"When did this happen? Why did this happen?" my dad demanded. I'd never seen him so out of sorts. Or red-faced. "Are you being serious right now?"

"George, stop yelling," my mom said. She then touched my hand. "Mari, please explain what you mean. Are you talking about a spiritual marriage? Did you marry yourself? Because you know I would've come to support you. You need to find yourself after"—her voice lowered to a whisper— "the David thing."

"You're pregnant!" Kate pointed her fork in my general direction. "That has to be it. Is it David's? Or do you not know? Oh my God, are you going on *Maury?* Please say yes. I want to be interviewed about how your baby daddy needs to pay child support."

That had been the last straw. Tossing my napkin onto my plate and standing, I said in a trembling voice, "I have to pee."

Now, here I was, staring in the mirror that I'd used for so many years as a teenager practicing my makeup. There was a dried bit of mascara on the bottom right corner that had never come off, and a nail polish stain on the counter. I traced the red smudge absentmindedly.

I almost wished I'd let Liam come with me. At least my

family could lob questions at him, too. But I'd thought it would be better to tell my family first before introducing him. When Liam had asked me where I was going tonight, I'd lied and said it was a work thing.

I hoped he'd bought it. The last thing I needed was an offended Irishman pouting when I got back home.

Home. Did I already think of Liam's apartment as home? It was really just the place where I was living, I reminded myself. In six months, I'd find a new apartment and forget all of this had happened.

Yeah right.

"Why did you tell your crazy family?" I muttered to myself as I washed my hands. But I knew I'd had to, because they would've found out anyway. Besides, Liam and I couldn't make this marriage seem real if we hid its existence from our friends and family.

"Mari?" said my mom's voice through the door. "Are you okay, sweetheart?"

Tears sprang to my eyes, which annoyed me. I wanted to tell my mom everything. I wanted to confess like I used to do as a kid, and she'd hug me and tell me I could make things right. *Mistakes are what make us grow,* she'd always say.

Sometimes I'd wanted to ask her if she'd felt like having a family had been a mistake. Because why else would she have left us without saying a word those two weeks? But as the years had passed, it had seemed less important to talk about that time. It was over. Time to move on.

I pushed the memories aside. I took a deep breath and opened the door, a trembling smile plastered on my face.

"I'm fine," I said way too cheerfully.

In her mid-fifties, Julie Wright was still an attractive

woman. She'd embraced her silver hair years ago and currently wore it in a French braid down her back that looked like a silvery snake. With her colorful shawls and propensity to meditate over crystals, she looked like a friendly witch—a witch who had run the financial side of our flower shop since my parents had opened it.

My mom portrayed herself as a woman who had her head in the clouds, but it was a facade. She was hella savvy. And she hadn't raised three daughters without learning when we were faking things.

My mom patted my hand. "Why don't you come back to the table? I told everyone to be quiet so you could explain."

"Thanks, Mom."

"Are you sure everything's all right? You're not in trouble?" She flicked her gaze to my midriff.

I had to stifle a giggle.

"Mom, no. I'm not pregnant. I swear. Besides, I'm twenty-nine, not nineteen. Getting accidentally pregnant wouldn't be the end of the world."

Well, except if I got pregnant with Liam's child, we'd never get away from each other.

Just the thought of being pregnant with Liam's baby made my heart race.

Oh, my stupid, stupid heart.

Except Liam didn't do commitment of any kind. He'd said as much multiple times. And babies were about as high on the commitment ladder as you could get.

"I guess that's true. But married, Mari? And not to David? And you didn't invite your family to the wedding?" said my mom.

My mom sounded so hurt that I had to hug her.

"I'm sorry. It was a sudden thing."

"You eloped?"

"More or less."

"Then you need to have a real wedding. You already have a dress and everything."

When I returned to the dining room, my dad looked decidedly uncomfortable. Kate had her hands folded in her lap, her gaze on her plate, which just made me more suspicious of her motives. My younger sister had some devious plan bouncing around in her head.

Dani and Jacob were talking to each other in low tones. I sat down, placing my napkin back into my lap.

Countdown to the first question:

Five, four, three, two—

"Who did you marry?" Kate burst out with. "And how? And why?"

My mom clucked her tongue. "Kate, don't interrogate your sister. She'll explain when she wants to. Be patient."

Kate had been born impatient. She'd been two weeks early, and my mom had almost given birth to her in the car because her labor had been so fast. My mom had always said that because Kate was a Sagittarius, she would always jump first, ask questions later. If she even cared enough to ask questions.

I was glad my mom had given me a moment to collect my thoughts. Liam and I had already discussed the story we were going to tell people regarding our marriage, and I had to remember the various details.

Firstly, Sam had introduced us, which was true. Secondly, we'd been dating for a few weeks, which of course wasn't true. Thirdly, when we were in Vegas, we'd decided to take the plunge because we were so in love. That one was the biggest lie of all. The only thing we felt for each other was lust with a side of frustration.

As I told the story to my family, I waited for someone to tell me I was lying, to point out some inconsistency Liam and I had missed. It didn't help that Dani wouldn't look at me the entire time, or that Kate looked at me with narrowed eyes, suspicion in her gaze.

I told myself I was protecting them. If they knew about how this wasn't a real marriage or how I was sticking it out solely for the money Liam had promised me, they'd lose their minds.

"Really lay it on," Liam had said wryly when we'd solidified the details of our story. "Make it sound like you're so in love with me you had to marry me on the spot."

"That's the only way anyone would believe I'd be that impulsive," I'd admitted.

"Exactly."

"Well, what about you? You'll need to say the same thing happened for you."

His lips had twisted into a strange smile, and he hadn't actually answered my question.

My family stared at me in silence after I'd told them the half-true, half-false story. I began to cut into my meatloaf, taking a bite of it, only to realize it had gone cold in the time I'd been in the bathroom. Cold meatloaf was one the least appetizing things on the planet.

"What do you know about this man? Because you knew David well, and look how that turned out," said my dad, crossing his arms.

"George. This was Mari's decision, and we should support

her. Besides, what's more romantic than eloping in Vegas?" said my mom.

"Marrying a man you actually know," countered my dad.

"It's like straight out of a romance novel. Did you lock eyes the second you first saw each other?" Kate widened her eyes until she looked almost ghoulish, the weirdo. "You took one look at Liam and you fell in love. Insta-love, basically. You didn't need to know anything about him because he was your *soul mate*. I totally ship this, you guys."

"Since when do you read romance novels?" said Dani.

"A girl has to find something to do on the weekends when she's single. Believe me, I'm not reading them for the plot."

"Young lady, behave yourself when we have company," said my dad.

Kate's lips lifted at the corners. "Jacob isn't company. He's family. So he should get used to the fact that I like to talk about how hung romance heroes are at dinner." She batted her eyelashes. "You don't mind, do you, Jacob?"

My dad sighed, covering his face with his hands in despair. Jacob had to cover his mouth with his napkin to hold back his laughter. Dani patted his arm as his shoulders shook. For me, I was just glad that Kate was taking the attention away from me.

"Thank you for sharing, Kate," said my mom. To me, she said, "When can we meet your husband? I don't know why you didn't bring him tonight."

Why hadn't I brought him? I realized how weird it seemed that I hadn't wanted to introduce my *husband* to my family yet. I tried to stall my answer by taking a bite of my now cold mashed potatoes, but they tasted like sand in my mouth. So much for eating at this family dinner. Tonight was a great night for late-night Taco Bell.

"I'll talk to him," I said finally, all the while knowing that if I had my way, I'd never talk to my husband again. Mostly so I didn't throw my panties at his head for a third time.

"Yes, we want to meet this man. Funny he didn't feel like coming tonight. Why is it my daughters keep dating men who I don't actually like?" said my dad, referring to his dislike of Jacob and his family. Although our parents had come around to the idea of Dani dating the son of our family's former rivals in the flower shop business, the truce between Jacob and our dad was still somewhat uneasy.

Jacob, at the reference to himself, shifted in his chair, looking irritated. Dani caught his gaze and mouthed something that soon smoothed the creases from his brow.

"I didn't tell Liam where I was going," I said, replying to my dad's question.

That earned me strange looks from everyone at the table. I wanted to poke my eyeballs out with my fork. It'd be better than the mixture of concern and confusion on my family's faces.

"You didn't tell your husband you were going to dinner," said my dad slowly. He turned to my mom. "How is this normal?"

"It's not like that," I said.

"He's not her keeper." This was from Dani. "I mean, I don't tell Jacob everything."

"You don't?" Jacob cocked an eyebrow. "Do elaborate."

"Why would I tell you when the whole point was that I *didn't* tell you?"

"I thought you were talking hypotheticals," said Jacob, who looked confused now.

Kate leaned forward. "You can tell me. You can tell me everything."

"There's nothing to tell!" said Dani.

I slumped in my chair, inwardly groaning.

This was also why I hadn't brought Liam. Because my family was *nuts*.

"Dani, do you have a secret?" My mom's eyes lit up. "Is there another reason why you got engaged so quickly?"

Apparently, my mom had grandchildren on the brain tonight. Since my uterus currently had an unoccupied sign, she hoped that Dani's didn't.

"Oh my God, there's no secret," said Dani. She was blushing. "And if you're implying that I'm pregnant—"

My dad hadn't been listening up until now, but now he barked, "Pregnant? Who's pregnant? If one of you is—"

"I am!" said Kate gleefully.

My dad started roaring like a bear while Kate laughed maniacally. Dani was trying to explain that Kate was joking, while Jacob kept asking Dani what she was keeping from him because now he was actually concerned.

My mom tried to intervene and eventually sighed, went into the kitchen, and returned with a bottle of wine.

"I think we're going to need this," she said. She poured me a glass before drinking hers in three gulps.

By the time I arrived home—no, not home, it was Liam's place—I stalled going inside. The entire drive home, anxiety churned in my gut. For the first time, this entire situation had truly dawned on me. It was like I'd been floating through a dream until reality had splashed me with a bucket of ice water.

I pressed my forehead to the steering wheel. That too-familiar panic threatened to take over like it had at Jenna's wedding reception. I took in a shuddering breath. Then another. Until I was calm enough to go inside and hope Liam wouldn't ask me about my supposed work party.

I wasn't talking to him anyway, so that should be easy enough.

Liam was lounging on the couch, music filling the living room. He had a spectacular view of Elliott Bay—way better than my view of a general store I'd had at my old place. The most exciting thing I'd see out my window was when raccoons would knock over the trashcans and the owner would come out, yelling at them and threatening to call the cops. I'd never had the heart to tell the owner there was no such thing as the raccoon police.

"Where were you tonight?" said Liam, stopping me in my tracks.

"I'm not talking to you right now."

"You just spoke words to me, so you seem capable."

He still hadn't even turned to look at me, like I wasn't worth his full attention.

In a snippy tone, I said, "I was at work. I told you that."

He tipped his head back to look at me finally. His eyes were dark, almost impenetrable. "It's funny, because I called your work and no one answered."

"Why were you calling my work?"

"I wanted to see if you wanted pizza. I texted you, but you never responded. So being the good husband I am, I called your work." He tilted his head back so I could no longer see his face. "So I'm curious: where were you?"

The stress of tonight compounded with Liam's interrogation was more than enough to snap my patience in two.

"What does it matter? It's none of your business. I don't know if you've forgotten, but we're not actually married. I don't have to tell you where I am at all times."

Liam rose from the couch. Soon I found myself being stalked toward the wall by over six feet of angry male.

"Where were you?" His voice was silky, and I could hear his accent lengthening the words. I knew his accent appeared more often when he was stressed or drunk—or angry.

"Because you look guilty, little wife. Were you with another man? Because I have to tell you, you don't get to mess around with somebody else when I'm not allowed to get any, either."

I couldn't breathe. The temperature in the room seemed

to increase until I felt sweat bead on my forehead. It took a second for Liam's words to filter in my brain. It was like he'd spoken them in Gaelic, and I had to translate them.

Another man. Liam thought I was *cheating* on him? Even though we weren't even together? Oh, he had balls of steel that I wanted to kick right now.

"Seriously? You're worried that I'm cheating on you? Good lord, where would I find the time, for one thing?"

He had the grace to look slightly abashed now. "When you didn't reply, I was…"

I waited three seconds before saying, "Worried? You were worried about me?"

"No. I was pissed that you were ignoring me."

He looked so perturbed, with not just me but with himself, that I couldn't stop myself from laughing at him.

Now he just looked confused. "The fuck are you laughing about?"

"You! You sounded so jealous and caveman-y, growling about me being with another man, when you couldn't just say you were concerned about me. Oh my God!"

Tears were streaming down my face now. "And I was just with my family. I wish I'd been with another man. That would've been preferable to getting grilled tonight."

At that, Liam's expression turned even pissier. "Your family?"

"Yeah, my family. I needed to tell them the story we concocted."

"Why didn't you just tell me that instead of lying?"

I blew out a breath, annoyed at myself and at him. "Because I didn't want to deal with your questions? Because I was afraid you'd be mad that I didn't want you to come? Because I'm losing my marbles? I don't know."

He pressed a hand against the wall, inches from my head. "Just tell me the truth and I'll tell you the same. Pretty easy, wife. Lying won't help either of us, especially when we have to lie to everyone else."

"Well, that sounds just so…logical. And it makes me want to like you." I sniffed.

He cocked an eyebrow. "Pretty sure you already like me plenty. I can always remind you, though."

Oh, he was smooth. He knew how to use my own words against me, too. I couldn't underestimate my husband, that was for sure.

"You also annoy me deeply," I added. "And I'm tempted to get back at you for accusing me of cheating on you."

Various forms of revenge passed through my mind. I thought of every way Kate had tormented me and Dani when we were kids. A frog in our beds, beetles in our shoes.

One time she'd shaved off Dani's eyebrow while she was sleeping. Dani had gotten her back by meticulously filling Kate's toothpaste with hemorrhoid cream. She'd used a tiny funnel and had spent at least two hours on that project.

As for me, Kate had put food coloring in my body wash, turning my skin blue. The blue tinge had lasted for over a week, and I'd had to wear long sleeves and pants in the middle of July.

I'd gotten her back when I hid a dead fish in her room. By the time she found it, her room smelled so awful she had to sleep on the living room couch for two weeks as her room aired out. Suffice to say that Kate didn't try to prank me again for a while after that.

But I couldn't put a dead fish in Liam's room, even though I was very tempted to. I was an adult. I had to revert to passive aggressiveness to get my revenge on annoying people. That was the mature way to do it.

"Any ideas?" said Liam, breaking through my reverie.

"I'm tempted never to replace the toilet paper so you're screwed when you have to poop, but that would be immature."

His lips twitched. "I'd just use one of your face cloths."

"Oh my God, gross!"

"You brought up pooping."

"I did, and it's my own fault. I'll think of something else, though. Just wait."

My mind, however, latched onto Liam's accusation that I'd cheated on him. It was ludicrous, and it also hurt. I might not have my life together, but I at least had my integrity. Well, barring the whole lying to my family thing.

I said quietly into the silence, "Do you really think I'd cheat—even if this isn't a real relationship—when I know how much that hurts? How deeply that betrayal cuts?"

"You're right. I wasn't thinking. I was already pissed about last night and then when you didn't respond…"

I said gently, "I'm sorry if you felt rejected last night. I just don't think getting involved is a good idea for either of us."

"Little wife," said Liam with a sigh in his voice, "I think we're way past that."

I groaned, because in this, my husband was right. "Why does sex have to make everything so complicated? With David. With you. It makes no sense."

"Because men are basically animals at the end of the day. We want sex; if we don't get it, we get riled up."

"Not *every* man."

"Ninety-nine percent of them, then."

"David wasn't like that." I didn't know why it mattered right then, or why I thought it was a good idea to tell my current, sort-of-fake husband about the man who was supposed to have been my real husband.

"He always told me he wasn't that into sex. But then he was afraid to initiate because I always turned him down. And he even bought us these buttons—"

I clapped a hand over my mouth. "Never mind. I shouldn't have said that. I'm going to bed."

Liam stopped me with a hand on my arm before I could slink off.

"You're not going anywhere until you explain that one. Buttons. Sex buttons? Was he into kinky shit?"

"Oh no. Nothing kinky. He didn't even like oral."

Liam looked—horrified. Like I'd told him David murdered old ladies for fun.

"You're telling me your ex didn't like having his cock sucked? You're fucking with me."

"I don't…I don't know." What did it matter at this point that I was talking about things I'd never wanted to discuss with anyone, though? I'd already gotten this far.

"We never did oral. It just wasn't anything either of us wanted to do. That's all."

"Sounds like bollocks to me. And you haven't answered my question, either."

"Fine, fine. David bought these buttons where if one person wanted sex, they could press one. The other person would only know if their partner wanted sex if they also pressed it. So nobody got their feelings hurt and felt rejected."

"Mari, baby," said Liam almost gently, "that is the stupidest fucking thing I've ever heard of."

"Is it? You were pretty mad last night when I rejected you."

Liam scowled. "I was mad that you were acting like you didn't want me when you obviously did. Besides, I'm man enough to have a woman tell me no when she truly means no. I'm not a monster. Sounds like this ex of yours was a fucking mess."

"Okay, fair point. But I did love David. I did. He was kind and caring until the whole cheating thing. He made me feel safe."

I crossed my arms over my chest, but Liam wasn't going to let me hide from him.

"You're safe with me." His voice was soft, almost like a caress. "Never doubt that."

I didn't know this man who was my husband, but I realized I was *getting* to know him. And something deep inside me believed him—or wanted to believe him, which was almost more dangerous.

He interrupted my thoughts to say, "But when you say you've never done oral…are you saying you've never had your pussy eaten? Ever?"

I flushed so hard I was probably going to burst into flames.

"Um, my first boyfriend in high school tried, but it was so awkward I made him stop. And with David, we just never did it."

To my shock, Liam kneeled on the ground, his head level with my crotch.

"Then we're going to fucking do something about that tragedy right now."

I didn't react, even when Liam began to unzip my jeans. I was too shocked—and honestly, too aroused. Seeing a man like him on his knees in front of me?

Maybe I *was* into some kinky shit.

"Your ex was a selfish piece of shit," said Liam, his voice rough. He palmed my mound through the silk of my panties. "A real man eats pussy."

I let out a giggle. "That should be your slogan."

"I could add it to my business cards. I'm sure I'd get a lot of new business from it."

I was about to reply when he kissed my pussy through the panel of my panties, shocked at the lust that shot through me so quickly.

With David, it had always taken forever to get me aroused. Then again, David had never put much effort into foreplay. I hadn't thought it was a bad thing because I'd always assumed that was just how sex was.

Explosive, passionate sex was just in fiction. Or porn. In real life, you had to temper your expectations.

"What if I don't like it?" I whispered.

"Then I'll stop." He flicked his gaze up to me. "Do you have a safe word?"

"No. Why would I?"

"Then you better choose one quick."

I racked my brain. Whatever happened to just saying *stop* or *no?* My brain could barely add two and two together with Liam starting to kiss the insides of my thighs, his beard rough against the sensitive skin there.

"Broccoli," I blurted.

"Pardon?"

"My safe word. Nobody says broccoli during sex. Right?"

"It's not my favorite choice of vegetable during sex, no."

"You use vegetables for sex—oh my God, what are you doing?"

Liam's smile was devious as he pulled my panties down to my knees before making me widen my stance.

"It's hard to eat pussy unless you let me get to the pussy in question, babe."

But with my shoes still on and my jeans and panties down at my ankles, it was awkward. With a growl, Liam helped me take everything off from the waist down.

"Put your leg on my shoulder." Liam wrapped his other arm around my ass to hold me still—or to hold me up, most likely. "Now show me this pussy."

I gulped. I could feel myself getting wetter just from his erotic words. I'd never felt so exposed, so lewd. Yet it only heightened my arousal.

I hesitated, though, and Liam picked up on it. "Want me to do it?" he said, so gently I wanted to cry.

"Yes. Please."

"My shy little wife. Let me see that pretty pink pussy."

He slowly parted my folds, displaying me fully. His gaze didn't waver as he took in that part of me that even David hadn't looked at. I couldn't breathe.

Liam slowly stroked a finger from my clit to right before my butt. He found the gathered moisture seeping from my sheath, groaning when it coated his fingers.

"Tilt your hips toward me," he said. "That's it. God, you're beautiful. Don't you know that? Your fiancé didn't deserve this tight little pussy. He should've been eating every day, morning till night."

"That sounds a bit excessive."

"How would you know?" Liam countered.

I whimpered, because he was right. I whimpered even more when Liam licked me from taint to clit, returning to thrust his tongue inside me. The sensation—how could I describe it? It was like I could feel his tongue along the entirety of my body.

He lapped at me then, sucking my juices into his mouth. He groaned when I began to quiver against his mouth. The feeling of his beard against my thighs, his warm tongue, his rough fingers—I wouldn't last.

How had I ever thought oral sex was awkward? I'd had no idea. I was like a virgin on her wedding night.

Cause of death: cunnilingus. Convicted killer: Liam Gallagher, pussy-eating champion.

I felt the orgasm building deep inside my belly. My nipples were painfully tight buds pressing against my bra, and I couldn't take in enough air. It was like stepping closer and closer to the edge of a cliff. Except instead of jumping and breaking my neck, it was jumping and losing complete control of my body.

Liam sucked my clit between his lips. Such a small thing, my clit, yet it seemed to contain an entire planet. And Liam was my sun, and I was caught in his orbit no matter how hard I tried to avoid it.

His dark head between my thighs, the sound of his tongue lapping at my pussy—all of it combined and suddenly my orgasm burst inside me. I cried out. Liam had to hold me up as I shook so hard I was pretty sure my bones had basically melted.

I'd be a jelly person for the rest of my life now solely from the best orgasm I'd ever been given.

"There you go," soothed Liam, kissing my thighs, petting my pussy as my release slowly tapered away. He then said something I didn't understand—something in Gaelic. He repeated the foreign word a second time before he kissed me hard.

I wanted to ask him what it meant, but Liam kissing me was too much of a distraction. I'd ask him later. Right now, I wanted very much to discover more about his body, especially the cock straining against his jeans.

And then the doorbell rang. We both jumped in surprise. The sound reverberated throughout the apartment.

Liam frowned. "Who the fuck is that?"

My brain was too melted to put together that the doorbell ringing meant a human being was outside.

"Maybe they'll go away," I ventured.

The doorbell rang a second time. Then a third. Then it was ringing like an alarm, *ding, ding, diiing, dingdingdiiiiiiiiiiiing.*

Liam swore and muttered to me, "Put your trousers back on," before marching to the door.

I managed to get my pants and panties back on before following Liam to the door. The doorbell stopped ringing when he wrenched the front door open.

"What the—" He stopped. I looked over his shoulder to see a young girl soaked to the skin right outside.

Through her chattering teeth, the girl said scathingly, "Took you long enough to open the door! I'm dying out here!"

CHAPTER THIRTEEN

"Niamh," I said, totally at a loss. "The bloody hell are you doing here?"

It was Mari who had the sense to usher my soaking-wet sister into the apartment. When had it started raining? *When you were licking your wife's pussy, that's when.*

"What's your name again?" said Mari to my sister.

"Niamh," said Niamh slowly, her teeth still chattering. "Like 'weave' except it starts with an 'n.'"

"It's nice to meet you, Niamh. Let's get you out of those wet clothes."

"I can do it myself," groused Niamh. "I know where the bathroom is. I don't even know who *you* are, though."

Niamh headed to the bathroom and shut the door hard enough that I winced.

What the hell was my teenage sister doing here? Did Uncle Henry and Aunt Siobhan know? It was a two-hour drive from Olympia, and it was a school night. There was no way they would've let her come here.

I checked my phone, only to realize the battery had died.

Plugging it in, the screen filled with missed calls and texts from my aunt and uncle.

Do you know where Niamh is? She's not answering her phone.

I sighed. My little sister must've got angry and driven here in a fit of teenage rebellion.

Just what I didn't fucking need.

"Sorry about this," I said to Mari, who was looking concerned as I scrolled through my phone. I realized I hadn't explained who Niamh even was. "She's my sister."

Mari's lips twitched into a smile. "I figured as much. She looks just like you."

"She does?" Niamh was small and delicate, where I was the opposite. The only physical traits we shared were our dark eyes and hair, and her hair was blue now. I shrugged. "I need to make some calls."

By the time I'd talked to Aunt Siobhan to assure her that Niamh was safe at my place, Niamh had emerged from the bathroom in Mari's robe. Mari was at least seven inches taller, so the robe trailed on the floor behind my sister like a queen's train.

"She just got here. Yeah. I don't know. We haven't got that far yet." I held out the phone to Niamh. "Aunt Siobhan wants to talk to you."

Niamh scowled. "Tell her I *don't* want to talk to her ever again."

Save me from dramatic teenage girls. Sighing, I conveyed the message, assuring our aunt that I'd take care of this and get Niamh back home as soon as I could, even if I had to drag her there myself.

Mari sat on the couch next to Niamh, her hands folded in her lap. It was hard to believe just a few minutes ago I had my mouth on her pussy, and she was coming against my tongue. She was still a little flushed from her orgasm. If Niamh hadn't interrupted us, we'd be in my bed and fucking six ways to Sunday.

I sat down in front of Niamh, giving her a stern look.

"How about you explain what the hell you're doing here?"

Niamh's bottom lip trembled. "I don't want to talk about it."

"You don't get to show up here in the middle of the night and not explain why."

Niamh tilted her chin up. "It's not the middle of the night. It's only ten-thirty."

"You don't get to be a smart-ass right now. Not when everyone is royally pissed with you."

"How pissed?"

"Aunt Siobhan sounded like she'd been crying, for one. She was freaking out. She was about to call the police and file a missing person's report."

Niamh went white. "It's only been a few hours!"

"You're a minor. Doesn't matter."

My sister crossed her arms over her chest, a mulish expression on her face. I saw Mari smile out of the corner of my eye.

When I shot my wife a look, her smile widened. "You guys look just like each other. Especially when you do that."

I realized both me and my sister were scowling, mirror images of each other.

In unison, we snapped, "No, we don't."

Niamh swiveled to face Mari. Her nose wrinkled. "Who are you exactly?"

I hadn't told Niamh about the Mari situation because how

did you explain that to a teenager? But I couldn't get out of it now. Great. Just fucking great.

Before I could explain, Mari said calmly, "I'm Mari. Your brother's girlfriend."

I had to mask my surprise that Mari called herself my girlfriend instead of my wife. Then again, she was wise to ease Niamh into this. I hadn't planned to tell Niamh about this thing at all. Now that she knew Mari was my girlfriend, our aunt and uncle would know, and the story would just get more complicated from there.

Niamh said to me, "He never told me he had a girlfriend. And we just saw each other. Wait, are you living here?" Niamh turned to me, incensed. "How could you not tell me about this? You never let girls move in with you. You said they get needy and want you to propose, and you don't believe in that shit—"

"Watch your mouth, young lady. I don't need to explain myself to you. You're the one who needs to explain why you ran away from home," I said.

"I don't want to talk about it."

I wanted to bash my head against the wall. Or maybe throttle my sister.

To my relief, Mari intervened to say, "Then maybe you should go to bed, and we can talk in the morning."

"I don't want to talk to you. You're not my mom," was Niamh's reply.

At that, I snapped, "Now you're just being a brat. Either be nice or you can go to bed, because you're not going to talk to Mari like that."

Niamh's eyes filled with tears. "I hate you!"

She went to the second bedroom and slammed the door shut with a bang.

Both Mari and I winced. Then I winced when I remembered all of Mari's stuff was in that room.

What a fucking disaster this was. And when did my seventeen-year-old sister become four again? It made zero sense.

"I'm sorry. She's usually not like this." I rubbed my jaw. I'd been clenching it so hard I could feel a headache forming. "She's usually more mature than this. I don't know what's going on."

"How old is she?" said Mari quietly.

"Seventeen. Too old to be throwing a fit, that's for sure."

"My sisters used to be like that when they were teenagers. Kate especially. She had a short temper, and when she got angry it was like a hurricane. My parents never knew what to do with her. It's easy to think teenagers are adults when they try hard to act like one."

"I can't imagine that you were like that, though."

Mari had a faraway look on her face. "No, but sometimes I wished I had been. I tend to keep my emotions locked down deeply. But they always come bubbling up eventually. That's why they're dangerous if you don't deal with them head on."

"It helps if you don't have any feelings, like me."

She rolled her eyes. "No one is more dead inside than the guy staying married to a woman he doesn't love solely for his sister's benefit."

"I'm not a hero." Looking Mari up and down, her cheeks still a little red from earlier, I added, "Besides, there are some benefits for me. It's not like you're forcing me to eat your pussy, sweetheart."

Mari shushed me and pushed at my shoulder. "Keep your voice down! And don't be gross."

"Not gross, just honest."

I wanted to haul her into my lap and kiss her, but I could hear Niamh pacing in her room. I didn't need my teenage sister to burst into the living room to see us making out. She'd never let me live it down. And she was in such a strange mood that it wasn't worth poking the hormonal, adolescent bear.

"I don't get it," I repeated, mostly to myself. "Niamh isn't usually like this. She's smart. Responsible. She's applying to Harvard and Yale and a bunch of other schools, for Christ's sake. She doesn't do stupid shite, which is why I haven't had to worry about her."

I felt the worry weigh down my shoulders. I was leaving Seattle after she got into university—that was the plan. Niamh would start university, and I could move on with my life. She would be an adult and have her inheritance, too.

And besides, I could hardly stay here when Mari would be living in the city. Seattle was big, but that didn't mean we wouldn't run into each other.

It was always easier to make a clean break of things.

And if my chest ached at the thought of never seeing Mari again? That was my own damn problem. More than likely it was from my never-ending case of blue balls where she was concerned.

"Where should I sleep tonight?" said Mari, breaking through my depressing thoughts. "I'm supposed to be your girlfriend now, according to your sister…"

I grimaced. *Shite, fuck, shite.* "You can sleep in my bed. I'll sleep on the floor."

"And what happens if Niamh sees you? She'll know something is up."

"I'll tell her we've taken a vow of abstinence."

Mari clucked her tongue. "What would you Irish say? 'Don't be daft?' We can share a bed."

"Sweetheart, if I'm lying in bed next to you," I said in my deepest Irish brogue, "I'm gonna put my cock in you."

"Then I'll wear my tightest Spanx to bed. No one can get them off of me. They're basically a chastity belt."

I moved closer to her until I could feel her breath puff against my chin. "I'd find a way, *a ghrá geal*. I can promise you that."

The endearment slipped from my tongue for the third time that night. When I'd first said it, I had barely realized it had come out of my mouth. *My bright one.*

I was a stupid arse for saying it again, because now Mari was going to keep asking me what it meant.

"I hope that means something nicer than that vampire monster woman you accused me of being before," she said.

I was about to lie through my teeth when Niamh came out of her room and said to Mari in the meekest voice I'd ever heard, "Can I borrow some pajamas? I forgot mine."

I wish I could say that Mari and I fucked when she stayed in my room that night.

But that would have made sense. That would've been what anyone would have expected. Even me. I hadn't lied when I'd said if she were in bed with me, I wasn't going to lie there like a chaste nun.

When I came into my bedroom and found Mari curled up on the right side, her red hair in a bun and her face clean of makeup, I went instantly hard.

Yet when I slid into bed next to her, she said, "We're not having sex."

My cock withered. "Why the fuck not?"

She gave me a look that could only be described as *wifely*. "This apartment is tiny. Your sister will hear us."

"Then you'll just have to be quiet."

Mari snorted. "Will it make you feel better if I say that there's no way I could manage to stay quiet?"

I could've beaten on my chest right then in triumph. "You aren't wrong," I rumbled. "I did make you scream. Multiple times."

"Scream is a bit hyperbolic. More like 'cry out.'"

"Sweetheart, call it whatever you like, but you just admitted that you can't keep quiet when I touch you. Which means I have to see how loud I can get you to be now."

Mari groaned. She yanked the covers to her shoulders and proceeded to tuck the blanket around her body like a butterfly in a cocoon.

"If you really don't want me to touch you," I said with a touch of asperity, "I won't."

"This isn't for you; it's for me."

I snorted. Punching my pillow, I lay down away from her, but it didn't help. I could hear every shift, every breath. I could *smell* her. She smelled like coconuts, and it annoyed me deeply. How the fuck was I supposed to avoid touching her when she smelled like being on holiday all the damn time?

"I'm gonna die from blue balls," I complained.

To which Mari replied, "Nobody dies from lack of sex. Stop complaining and go to sleep."

Despite my wife's command, I didn't sleep a wink that night. My only consolation was that when she got up, she looked as tired as me.

While Mari got ready for work, Niamh emerged from her room, yawning widely.

"It's so early!" she whined. "Why are you guys awake?"

"Some people have to go to work. And you should be in school. In case you forgot," I said.

"It's just one day."

"You're graduating soon. You can't be skipping school, Niamh. How the hell are you gonna get into Harvard or Yale or wherever if you do shite like this?"

Niamh didn't answer. Instead, she headed to the kitchen and began to scrounge around like a raccoon. I was drinking my first cup of coffee, staring out onto foggy Elliott Bay, when I heard crunching noises behind me.

"You gonna tell me why you drove all the way here?" I said finally.

Niamh sighed. "It's all Aunt Siobhan's fault."

Aunt Siobhan was a hard-ass, but she wasn't cruel. Niamh, though, had a tendency to push boundaries. I'd probably given her her way too often when she'd been little, especially once I'd realized how attached she was to me.

When she'd get upset that I was going somewhere, I'd let her come with me as often as I could. When she'd wanted to sleep in my bed with me, I'd given in and let her. Between working all the time and caring for my little sister, it wasn't like I'd been knee-deep in women anyway. Now, though, Niamh had the expectation that she'd always get what she wanted.

"We got into a fight on Monday," began Niamh between crunches of cereal. "I bought this top at the mall, and I was going to wear it to school. But Aunt Siobhan freaked out. She said it was way too tight."

Niamh scowled. "It wasn't *that* tight. And it's not like I have boobs so I didn't have tons of cleavage. Girls at school wear way worse things."

"You're telling me you ran away over a piece of clothing?"

Niamh flushed. "No! It was what it represented."

"Oh, now we're getting symbolic."

"You don't get it. Aunt Siobhan keeps trying to control me. Everything I wear, say, do—she doesn't like it. If I wear a dress that's above the knee, she acts like I've killed someone. If I stay out past eleven, she freaks out and thinks I'm gonna do drugs or have sex. She even went through my closet a month ago and threw out all the clothes she thought were slutty."

Niamh's lower lip trembled. "She says it's because I never go to mass with her anymore. That I'll end up being like one of those bad girls. Which is so unfair! My grades are perfect! I don't even do anything bad—not really, anyway. It's not like I'm getting pregnant after school!"

"Why would Aunt Siobhan think you're sleeping with someone?"

Niamh stared out the window, her face as red as a cherry. "There's a boy," she mumbled.

Of course there was. I should've fucking known. I turned my sister toward me and lifted her chin, "Am I going to have to kill somebody, Niamh? Has some boy touched you?"

"No! Oh my God! It's not like that. We've only gone on a few dates."

The puzzle pieces began clicking together inside my brain.

"And you did it behind Aunt Siobhan's back," I supplied.

Niamh scowled. "Because it's a stupid rule that I can't date. I'm not dumb enough to let a boy ruin my life, but Owen, he's different. He's not like that. And I really, really like him."

"So you fought over a boy, got mad, and drove here. Why? Did you think I'd pat you on the back for messing around with a boy when you should be focusing on school? I'm not going to support you being an idiot, throwing away your future like this."

"I'm not throwing anything away!"

"You're not acting like you aren't."

Tears formed in Niamh's eyes. "I should've known you wouldn't understand. You're just like Aunt Siobhan. You think you can control me, that you can tell me what I should do with my life. It's not fair! Why can't any of you trust me?"

"Behaving like this? Why should we trust you? You're acting like a brat, Niamh. Grow up."

My sister's chin trembled. A sob burst from her, and then she stormed off right as Mari emerged from the bathroom. A moment later, the front door slammed closed.

"What in the world?" said Mari. "Are you going after her?"

"Why should I when she's acting like that?"

"I'm not sure calling her a brat is going to help."

I scowled, just like my sister had done a few moments ago. First my sister, now my wife?

"Then you go after her, if you think you know how to handle her. If she wants to ruin her life, that's her problem."

"You're both idiots," Mari muttered right before she went after my sister, leaving me to stew alone.

CHAPTER FOURTEEN

MARI

Running after a teenager wasn't exactly in my plans this morning, but here I was, on the streets of downtown Seattle, trying to catch up to Niamh.

Liam hadn't told me much about his sister beyond her aspirations to get into an Ivy League. He'd said she wanted to study political science and to start a non-profit.

"Why am I the one doing this?" I said to myself, startling a man walking past me. Liam should be the one here, not me.

I could see Niamh and her blue hair up ahead, about a block away. I walked faster, almost running when I saw the WALK sign turn on.

"Niamh! Wait!"

Niamh glanced over her shoulder, scowled, and walked faster.

I was considerably taller than Liam's sister, my legs longer, and luck was on my side when Niamh got caught in a crowd of fanny-pack wearing tourists most likely walking to Pike Market.

Why anyone would come to Seattle in January, I had no idea. Maybe they were actual masochists. Based on their shorts and sandals, they were either insane or robots who didn't care about freezing to death.

Niamh knew when she'd been caught: cars were zooming past on the street, and the crowd took up the entirety of the sidewalk. Her shoulders sagged when I finally got to her.

"Seriously? Where's my brother?" She crossed her arms over her chest.

"He's sitting at home, pouting, rather like you're doing right now."

Niamh snorted. "My brother doesn't pout."

"Oh yes he does. You both do. He was making that same face when I left."

"Good. I hope he's crying, too."

"You're probably being too hopeful on that point."

A tourist jostled us both. It was cold; the mist was increasing to the point that my hair was going to turn into a total frizz ball. I wasn't going to attempt a conversation out in the middle of downtown Seattle.

"Let's get some coffee," I said.

"Don't you have to go to work? That's why you and Liam were up so early." Niamh looked a bit too triumphant, remembering that detail.

Shit. Well, this was a family emergency, right? Keeping my husband's sister from running off again?

"We're getting coffee," I said firmly. To my relief, Niamh followed me without protest to the coffee shop across the street.

After I'd made a quick, apologetic phone call to Leslie,

telling her I was going to be late this morning—*no, not sure how late, it was a family crisis, I'm so sorry*—I bought coffee for both me and Niamh. I also got two giant chocolate croissants, because this was a situation that called for baked goods.

Niamh slumped in her chair across from me. Now having the time to really study her, I could see how young she was. I knew she was seventeen, of course, but kids her age were rather talented at acting like they were already adults, like I'd said to Liam last night. I remembered that when I was her age I was convinced I knew everything. The adults around me were the ones who were idiots.

I ate my croissant and drank my coffee, waiting for Niamh to speak first. Having grown up with younger sisters—and considering Kate was only a few years older than Niamh—I knew it was better to let them talk when they wanted to talk.

And why do you care so much? She's not going to be your sister-in-law for much longer, my mind whispered. *Why get involved?*

Why, indeed. If I looked too closely at the reasons why, I'd probably throw myself into Elliott Bay right this second.

My phone beeped, alerting me to a text from Liam.

Where are you two? Did you catch up to Niamh? I'm on my way if you'll tell me where you are.

We're at a cafe. You don't need to come. I'll talk to her, I replied.

The blue dots pulsed on the screen for a long moment, as if Liam wasn't sure how to respond. Then he finally texted, *Thank you. I owe you big time.*

"Was that my brother?" said Niamh.

"Yes. He's worried about you."

"I don't want to talk to him."

"I figured. I told him to stay home for now."

The stubborn set to Niamh's jaw softened, but not before she narrowed her eyes at me.

"Who are you, again? I mean, is my brother really dating you? His girlfriends have never cared about me."

I wished I could tell her the truth, but Liam had wanted to keep our marriage a secret from his sister. But there was something ridiculous about that fact that I was here because of her, and she didn't even know. How was that for irony, huh?

"I'm your brother's girlfriend," I said finally.

"Yeah, I know that. But he's never had a girlfriend. I mean, not one that sticks around long. He's never let a woman live with him, either." Niamh's gaze sharpened. "Are you knocked up?"

I choked on my coffee. My eyes streaming, I coughed. To my surprise, Niamh got up and returned with a glass of water.

"Don't die on me," she muttered.

I drank the water, wiping my eyes. "No, I'm not pregnant," I croaked.

"So my brother just *likes* you?"

Niamh looked so stumped that I let out a laugh.

"It seems like that's the case."

"Huh." She began to pick at her croissant, the pastry flakes getting all over the table. "I think the longest he's dated any woman was two months. That was a long time ago, though. He's moved around so much that there was no point to having anything long-term. Or so he always told me."

"Are sisters usually this interested in their brothers' love lives?"

Niamh screwed up her nose. "I'm not *that* interested. I don't need to know the details. But I know Liam. I've known him way longer than you. He doesn't do commitment."

My stomach twisted, even though I already knew that. I knew this thing was just a ploy, a means to an end. But that didn't help the rock that formed in my stomach.

I said quietly, "I know."

Niamh looked nonplussed. "Well. Okay then."

Desperately needing to change the subject, I said, "Liam says you've applied to a bunch of Ivy League schools."

Niamh looked surprised. "He talks about me?"

"Of course. You're his sister."

Right then, she looked like a little girl as she said, "He doesn't act like he cares. I barely see him. Maybe once every six months. And he's moving away from Seattle when I go to college, anyway."

"You'll be moving away, too, though," I said gently.

"I'll still come back to see my aunt and uncle, and I'd see my brother, too." Niamh scowled. "Although maybe I won't go see my aunt and uncle, if they keep acting like assholes."

"It sounds like they just want to protect you."

"I get that. I'm not stupid. But it's not fair, because I haven't done anything for them not to trust me. Aunt Siobhan just assumes that if I so much as look at a boy, I'll end up pregnant."

Niamh crossed her arms, her pose so reminiscent of Liam that my heart ached. "I wanted to get on birth control, and she had a shit-fit. Acted like I was going to murder babies and old people for fun. And when I said it wasn't even for sex, she didn't believe me. So now I'm tempted to have sex just to piss her off."

"My younger sister Dani had the same issue when she was your age," I said, remembering the epic fights Dani and my dad had had when she'd wanted to go on birth control. "Her periods were all over the place, but our dad was not okay with the idea. It took our mom to talk him down."

I thought back to when I'd come home for the summer after my freshman year of college, and Dani was locked in her room after a huge fight with our dad. He'd caught wind of her idea to go on birth control and had vehemently refused to let her. At the time, I'd thought he was being absolutely ridiculous. Besides, it wasn't his body. I'd told him as much.

But now I understood it, to some degree. He'd been scared, and he'd reacted poorly. He had eventually apologized to Dani, although it had taken longer for her to forgive him.

"Look, I don't know your aunt or your uncle, of course, but they've basically raised you, right? I'm going to guess they're freaking out, in a general sense."

"Why? I haven't done anything to make them freak."

"Besides running away? And I'm gonna guess, dyeing your hair?"

"Oh, Aunt Siobhan was so mad when she came home and found out I'd done this to my hair." Niamh fingered the blue strands. "I was grounded for a month, but it was worth it."

If I were Niamh's mother, I'd be losing my mind, too. Teenagers were such terrors.

"They're probably also freaking out because you're growing up. You're going away for college. Soon they'll have to let you go out on your own completely. They can't protect you forever, no matter how much they want to."

"They don't get to dictate my life."

I took a deep breath. "I agree." Niamh shot me a surprised look. "I'm more inclined to agree with you, based on what you've told me. But your story is also pretty biased, I'm sure."

Niamh stared at me, slowly uncrossing her arms. "You're on my side? You don't even know me."

"Maybe, but I've been in your shoes, in a way. My sisters have been, too." I put up a finger. "That being said, you can't run off when you get mad. If you want to be treated like an adult, you're going to have to act like one. Losing your temper at the drop of a hat is not how you show that."

Niamh didn't have anything to say to that.

"I'm not a brat, though," she said quietly. "Liam just doesn't get it, either. He's just like Aunt Siobhan."

I snorted. "You and your brother are both exactly the same. You react without thinking. If you'd both take a deep breath, you'd probably not end up yelling at each other."

Niamh's lips curled in the first smile I'd seen from her. Even with her hair in a messy ponytail and wearing a sweat-shirt and torn jeans, she was lovely. I could see why Liam worried about her: she'd have to fight boys off with a stick, besides the fact that she was so headstrong.

Then her dark-eyed gaze swiveled toward me, doing that probing thing that Liam was way too good at.

"You're not like any of the other girls my brother's dated, you know."

"Is that a good thing or a bad thing?"

"Both. Neither." Niamh shrugged. "For one, he's never let any of them so much as talk to me, let alone do something like this. That means he trusts you. Liam doesn't trust anybody."

My heart squeezed, but I masked the rush of euphoria with a sip of my latte. Which had gone lukewarm while I was talking.

"And then last night, he kept looking at you. Like he needed you for something." Niamh tapped her chin. "It was weird. I kept waiting for him to ask you a question, but he didn't."

"Was he looking at me?" I hadn't noticed; I'd been too focused on the sudden appearance of his sister.

"Yeah. He was. A whole lot. But then I couldn't help but notice that my bedroom is full of *your* stuff. Not only that, but like someone had been sleeping in the bed recently." Niamh sipped her own coffee with a faux innocent expression. "Which is weird, don't you think? For two people supposedly in love?"

This girl was too smart by half. Or just too observant. I wanted to tell her the truth, but she was Liam's sister. He'd feel like I'd betrayed his trust—that trust Niamh was sure that I'd already gained—if I blabbed our entire story.

"We'd been fighting," I hedged, which wasn't exactly untrue. "I slept in that room the night before. If I'd known you were coming, I would've changed the sheets."

"Uh-huh."

How had she turned the tables on me? Needing to end this subject as soon as possible, I got up from the table. But I did it too quickly: I overset my coffee, spilling it across the table.

"For the love of God," I muttered, attempting to grab a bunch of napkins from a nearby dispenser, only to realize it was empty except for a single napkin. I turned to find another dispenser, but I failed to see the woman behind me. I jostled her, her coffee spilling over the side of her mug.

"Watch it!" the woman said, holding her coffee above her head now. "This is hot!"

Niamh was giggling, and I was blushing like crazy. Feeling beyond stupid, I managed to find some napkins, cleaned up the mess I'd made, and said to Niamh, "We're going home."

"Probably a good idea. Should I hold your hand? I don't want you to fall into a manhole or anything," said Niamh.

For the first time in my life, I had to restrain myself from giving a teenager the middle finger.

I paced the length of my flat while Mari and Niamh were gone. I reconsidered at least twenty times if I should go after them. Niamh was *my* sister. She'd been my responsibility since the moment she'd been born.

Yet Mari hadn't minced words in her texts. Stay home; you'll make things worse.

It pissed me off. I wanted to go straight to that cafe and prove Mari wrong. Pull up a chair, plant my arse in it, and force Niamh to talk to me.

Right as I debated leaving, my phone rang. Thinking it might be Mari, I answered it without looking at the caller ID.

The voice on the other line, though? Definitely not a woman's voice. It was a voice I'd only heard a half dozen times in my life, but I'd never forget it.

"Liam," said old man Gallagher in that Irish brogue that instantly took me back to my days in Dublin. "How are you?"

My grandda had called me once before here in the States to tell me I was getting a tiny percentage for my inheritance while Niamh was getting the rest.

"Did you really call to chat?" I said.

My grandda chuckled, dry as sandpaper. "You always were a rude lad. No, I didn't want to chat. I wanted to wish you many happy returns on your marriage."

You know that feeling when you can feel shite about to fall on your head but it hasn't happened quite yet? The ax before it falls on your neck. The step before your foot lands in dog shite. That feeling.

"I was surprised you didn't call to tell me you were engaged," continued old man Gallagher. "I would've sent you a gift."

"What, a severed head?" I said dryly.

Old man Gallagher tsked. "Manners. I hope she's a good Catholic girl."

I had no idea if Mari was Catholic or not, which was a strange realization right then. Shouldn't I know if my wife practiced a particular religion?

"I hope you make certain you're married in the eyes of the church. 'Tis important, like."

"Or what?"

"You take everything as a threat, don't you?" Switching to Gaelic, old man Gallagher added, "I just hope you know what you're doing. That's all. Have a lovely day, and tell my granddaughter I said hello."

He hung up on me before I could tell him to go to hell. Swearing long and low, I sat down heavily on the couch.

He knew about my marriage. And if he knew about the marriage, he'd know quickly enough if it wasn't legitimate. Hell, I should probably look into getting the Church's blessing just to be safe. My grandda was a kook, but he was a devout one.

I wasn't stupid enough to think that hadn't been a veiled threat. Old man Gallagher was on the scent, and, like a bloodhound, he wouldn't give up until he had his jaws around my throat.

Well, as much as a man who only came up to my shoulder could sink his teeth into me. It was like having an evil leprechaun biting at your ankles, except this leprechaun could hurt Niamh way more than he could hurt me.

I didn't get the chance to see my sister or Mari again until that evening. I'd had to photograph a couple down at Gas Works Park, which was great in the summer but froze your balls off in the winter. The woman had complained the entire time about being cold, while her fiancé had told her she shouldn't have worn a strapless dress and heels in January.

By the end of the shoot, I'd seriously contemplated pushing them both into Lake Union. If that was what marriage meant, I didn't want anything to do with it.

Yet when I walked into my flat and saw Mari putting makeup on my little sister, the two of them laughing like actual sisters, I wondered how the hell I'd be able to let Mari go in less than six months.

Niamh went rigid when I came inside, but Mari tilted Niamh's chin up and effectively distracted her. "Keep your head there."

"It's giving me a crick in my neck," whined Niamh.

"Having a line of foundation on your jaw would be worse. Don't move."

I watched Mari work in fascination. I'd seen her do her own makeup a few times, but the way she managed to transform my sister was nothing short of astonishing. Mari's skill was enough that Niamh didn't look ridiculous despite the dark lipstick and fake eyelashes.

Niamh held up the mirror, her eyes widening. "Oh, I love it! What did you do to make my nose skinnier?"

"Nothing a little contouring can't fix," said Mari.

Niamh kept looking at all angles of her face, getting so close to the mirror that she left a smudge on the glass. "I look pretty," she marveled.

"You are pretty," I rumbled. "Even without makeup."

Niamh blushed and turned toward me. "Are you going to be nice to me now?"

"Only if you're nice to me."

Mari shot me a look. "Niamh, how about you clean up here while I talk to your brother?"

I found myself hustled into my bedroom. "Don't provoke her again," said Mari in exasperation.

"Provoke *her?* She's the one who threw a fit."

"Because she's seventeen."

"Old enough to know better."

"Yes, but knowing isn't as simple as *doing.* You can't tell me you weren't an idiot at that age, either."

When Mari crossed her arms under her breasts, giving her some nice cleavage, I didn't feel particularly inclined to discuss my sister anymore. With Niamh here, it was like we had to act like actual nuns, despite the fact that we were supposed to be dating in Niamh's mind. How was that for fucking complicated?

I thought of old man Gallagher's phone call earlier, and it shot my lust down like a bullet. If he found out that Niamh was running away from home along with this whole fake marriage with Mari... My gut tightened.

"I need to tell you something," I said quietly.

In low tones, worried that Niamh would listen at the door like the brat she was, I told Mari about old man Gallagher calling and his veiled threat. Mari turned pale, not asking any questions until I'd finished.

I sat down on the end of the bed. "I'm sorry to rope you into all of this," I said heavily. "You didn't sign up for my fucking insane family."

Mari sat down next to me, and to my surprise, took my hand.

"No, but my family is just as crazy in its own way." She hesitated a breath before adding, "I'd like you to meet them some time. They're basically chomping at the bit to know who you are."

Her fingers were warm and slight, curled against mine. I hadn't yet got her a ring—too busy with everything going on.

Brushing my thumb across her ring finger, I said, "What kind of ring do you want?"

"I thought we weren't doing that. There's no reason to spend the money."

"What kind?" I pressed.

I smiled when it took all of one second for her to blurt, "Morganite with a rose gold band."

"I'm thinking that's not the ring your ex got you."

Her lips twitched. "He bought me a very nice diamond."

"Boring, colorless." I touched her jaw before stroking a length of her bright hair. "You're neither of those things."

"Oh, I'm as boring as they come."

Her skin was fine as silk. When I discovered a tiny mole behind her left ear, I wanted to kiss it. "You're the least boring woman I've ever met."

"I don't believe that."

"Believe what you want, wife. No boring woman would've married me in Las Vegas on a whim."

Her breathing increased as I stroked her throat. I liked to watch her pulse beat faster.

"I was drunk," she said breathily.

"I would've done it even if I hadn't been rat-arsed."

Her eyes widened to saucers. I wished instantly I hadn't admitted that. *You bloody idiot. What the fuck is she gonna think now?*

A knock on the door jolted us both out of our thoughts.

"Are you guys still having sex? Because I'm starving and there's nothing to eat here," whined Niamh.

Mari laughed as I stalked to the door, opening it to show that we were both clothed. "We're just talking, you little brat."

"Or you just finished super early." Niamh's smile was evil. "Only ten minutes, Liam? For shame."

"Go to your room. Now," I said darkly.

"Don't get mad. There are ways to fix that problem, you know."

Why had I given a fuck about my sister? She was a menace to society. She needed to be locked up for my own sanity.

"Go to your room before I strangle you," I rumbled.

Niamh shrugged. "Before you kill me, can you order some food first? I'm starving."

IT HAD TAKEN ANOTHER DAY, but I'd finally got Niamh to agree to speak with Aunt Siobhan about their fight. But not before we'd had our own heart-to-heart.

Look, I wasn't into touchy-feely conversations where you cut out your heart and cry. Why talk about a thing when you could do something about it?

"You can't solve this for her," Mari had said the night prior to my conversation with my sister. "She has to come to the decision herself."

I'd punched my pillow. "She's not good at making her own decisions."

"She'll only rebel if you try to control her."

Mari had rolled over, her back to me, and my cock had stirred. Why were we not having sex? She was in my bed, wearing her pajamas. It would take all of five seconds to strip off her trousers and have my hands down her panties.

Because she said she doesn't want to sleep with you. Remember?

Yeah, I was definitely going to change that. Besides, I'd already eaten her pussy, tasted her orgasm on my tongue. She could act like it hadn't happened as long as she wanted, but I caught her looking at me from the corner of her eye when she thought I wouldn't notice.

I saw the way her pupils dilated when I came close to her. The flush that climbed her cheeks. Her nipples were little beads every time I so much as breathed.

Mari, Mari, quite contrary. Your lips say one thing, but your body says another.

But seduction could wait until I got my sister back home. So I'd told my cock to cool it, had turned away from my overly fastidious wife, and had tried to sleep.

"Niamh, we need to talk," I said in the morning.

Niamh scowled. "No, thanks."

"It wasn't a question."

She continued eating her bowl of cereal like she hadn't heard me.

Then: "Why should we talk when I know exactly what you're going to say? 'Niamh, you can't date. Niamh, you need to go home. Niamh, you're too young to know what you want.' Blah, blah, blah."

She was so accurate that it irritated me further.

"You can't stay here," I said lamely.

I had her there; she couldn't exactly graduate if she didn't attend school. But she just shrugged one shoulder in pure adolescent apathy.

"Let's go for a walk," I said. "And that's not a request. Get your coat."

Niamh sighed, but she did as I asked. Although it was mid-January now, the sun peeked out from the clouds. I could smell the salt from Elliott Bay, and occasionally a brisk wind would blow straight through my coat.

Seattle reminded me of Ireland sometimes—the green, the gloom. The mists that would settle over the city like a gentle blanket. Sometimes I could almost imagine I was back in Dublin, until I heard the sounds of flat, American accents. Americans loved to say that everything was *awesome*. It was their favorite word, besides *freedom* and *super-sized*.

"You can't stay here," I said as Niamh and I walked to nowhere in particular.

She sighed, her breath huffing like smoke. "I know."

"You need to work this out with Aunt Siobhan. She keeps calling me, asking how you're doing. She's worried sick."

Niamh hunched into her scarf. "She shouldn't have been such a jerk," she mumbled.

"Maybe, but you didn't need to lose your temper, either.

You can't run every time things get tough. Because then you'll be running away your entire life."

"And what about you? You're always leaving."

I stopped, a man behind me almost running into my shoulder. He muttered something and stepped around me.

"What the hell does that mean?" I demanded.

"You've never stayed in one place for more then, what, a year? You don't want me to live with you, ever. You don't believe in commitment. You said so yourself."

"I'm with Mari now," I said, hating that I was using her in this argument.

"Yeah, maybe you are. For now. But then you'll up and move because you say you're bored or whatever. You've been doing it my entire life."

"Niamh, I've never abandoned you."

"No? You dropped me off on our aunt and uncle's porch and then I didn't see you for six months."

When I'd been twenty, new to America and trying to make a decent life for myself, I'd taken Niamh to the best place I knew of. She'd been young enough that I'd assumed she would adjust to her new home.

It had killed me to do it. That day would be imprinted on my mind for the rest of my life. Hugging my sister goodbye, telling her in Gaelic to be good, and then leaving. She hadn't cried or run after me, because she hadn't understood I wouldn't be coming back.

When I'd finally had the money to see her again six months later, she'd seemed perfectly happy. Well-adjusted. Her Irish accent had already faded significantly. As far as anyone knew, she was just a normal American child attending public school and saying that everything was awesome.

Niamh's eyes filled with tears as people maneuvered around us.

"Why did you leave me?" she asked in a soft voice.

"Oh, sweetheart." I took her hands and then enfolded her inside my coat. "I thought it was the best for us both. I was too young; I didn't know how to raise a child. I didn't have the means, either. How could I have dragged you around the country? That would've been hell for you."

"Not if I'd been with you."

Well, if I thought my heart was dead, it wasn't now. Guilt assailed me.

"So why did you run away? I don't understand," I said.

"I don't know." Niamh sniffled and pulled away. "I've always felt like no one wanted me, that's all. Aunt Siobhan acts like I'm a burden. She always has."

"That's not true."

"How would you know? You haven't been there."

"I'm sorry. I'll be better. But believe me: you were never unwanted. You're my sister. I'd do anything for you."

Even stay married to a woman who doesn't want me.

"Okay," whispered Niamh. "You'll call more?"

"Yes."

"And come see me?"

"If I can."

"And let me come to Seattle whenever I want?"

"If everyone agrees, yes."

She hugged me then, right there in the middle of downtown Seattle. But it was brief, the kind of hug you don't plan to do and feel a bit embarrassed about afterwards.

We didn't talk while we walked home. Niamh seemed deep in thought, and I had my own emotions to deal with.

I'd been so focused on my own life, my career, my financial situation, that I'd told myself I didn't need to burden Niamh with those things. She was taken care of, I'd told myself. I'd done what Mam had asked me to do.

But I'd failed somehow. It was a bitter pill to swallow.

"I'm going to call Aunt Siobhan," said Niamh after we'd returned to the flat "I'll go home tomorrow, too."

After Niamh went to her room, I sat down next to Mari on the couch.

"Well, I guess you worked things out," she ventured.

She looked so beautiful, sitting there in just sweats and a tank top, her hair in a bun, that it physically hurt to look at her.

"I don't want to talk about it," I said gruffly.

And because my wife was the most remarkable woman I'd ever met, she only said, "Okay," took my hand in hers, and sat with me in companionable silence.

Niamh left the next day, but not before Liam had made her promise to behave herself.

"You're giving me gray hairs already," he'd said when she'd hugged him.

"You'll look dashing with a salt and pepper look." Niamh had turned to me, and to my surprise, had hugged me tightly. She'd whispered in my ear, "Take care of him? He's stupid but I love him anyway."

I'd just nodded. That moment last night, when Liam and I had sat in silence, had changed something between us. It had been a silence loaded with intimacy, with emotions, with things that were dangerous but heady at the same time.

Returning to his apartment, we lapsed into silence again. We hadn't been truly alone in three days—not since the night he'd given me the greatest orgasm I'd ever had.

Sleeping next to him without really *sleeping* with him? That had been pure torture. His smell, his heat, the way he looked while he slept. His hair tousled in the morning, or how he stretched and showed off every muscle without even realizing it.

At the moment, Liam wore a blue sweater that looked way too good on him. He hadn't shaved this morning. He looked like a pirate, like he'd toss you over his shoulder and ravish you while smiling that devilish smile that melted your panties right off.

"So," he said.

I jumped. I was so startled I nearly dropped the cup of coffee I'd just picked up.

"Careful." Liam caught me, setting the coffee down. "Let's not injure ourselves anymore, eh?"

"Probably a good idea."

He hadn't taken his hand from mine, and the heat of his fingers was searing. And then I stared at his mouth, and memories of the way he'd licked my pussy spread through me like flames. I felt myself growing wet simply from the memory of his touch. How was that for unfair?

"We're alone," he rumbled. "Bloody finally."

"Yes."

"Sleeping next to you every night has been fucking with my brain. And my cock. Every night, I go to bed hard and every morning I wake up hard."

I swallowed, my mouth dry. "That doesn't sound fun."

"No, it's not fun, wife. Not with your gorgeous arse inches away, tempting me. Or the way you sigh in your sleep, or how your shirt rides up until I can almost see your breasts."

"Oh God, seriously?"

"I wasn't complaining."

Why had I said we shouldn't have mind-blowing, panty-flaming sex? Clearly I was deranged. Unhinged. My pussy felt sad and neglected. It probably could file a police report with how I'd been treating it lately.

Mari won't let a sexy Irishman touch me. She's so mean.

"Tell me to leave you alone," growled Liam as he backed me against the kitchen counter, "tell me to go, Mari. And I'll never touch you again."

I should say no. I should resist.

Be strong, Mari. There lies heartbreak.

But when it came to Liam Gallagher, the husband I'd never thought I'd have, I wasn't strong. I didn't want to resist him. Because he'd somehow managed to find a place inside my heart. I knew I could run to the other side of the world, and he'd still be foremost in my head.

"No, don't leave me alone. Please don't leave me alone," I said, looping my arms around his neck. "I need you."

He groaned. Picking me up, he kissed me at the same time he walked us to his bedroom. No, *our* bedroom. Somehow in the space of three days, it had become just as much my space as his.

"I can't be gentle," he said as he sat me down. "I want you too badly."

Gentle lovemaking would probably break me in half, anyway.

"Fuck me, Liam. I need it."

His eyes darkened until they looked black. His hands were everywhere: my back, my ass, my breasts. He cupped my pussy and pressed his palm against me, making me squirm.

"You're like an inferno. Are you already soaking for me, little wife?"

I couldn't speak when he rubbed my clit through the fabric of my jeans and panties. The roughness was enough to make me come, but before my release slammed into me, he moved his hand away. I whimpered.

"You aren't coming until you're on my cock. Your tight pussy clenching around me like a vise."

"Oh my God."

Liam licked my neck before he stripped me of my shirt. Unsnapping my bra, he feasted on my breasts for a long moment. He pinched my nipples until the pain bloomed into pleasure, until they were red and aching. When he swirled his tongue around one, I could only hang onto him or I would've collapsed onto the floor.

Every time Liam had touched me, I'd realized how little I knew about sex. I might not have been a virgin, but I'd never had sex like this. And we hadn't gotten to the main event yet. The thought of him plunging inside me made me tremble in anticipation.

Liam stepped away. My breasts were aching, heavy. I looked down to see beard burn across my fair skin.

"Strip for me. I want to see everything my wife has to offer me."

"Only if you strip, too."

He grinned. "As you command."

He took off his shirt, and I stood rooted to the spot. I'd seen his bare chest before, but once again I couldn't help but marvel.

He was like a marble statue. But warm, and alive, and when I placed my hand over his sternum, I felt the heavy beat of his heart.

And God, I wanted to see his cock. To feel it in my hands,

to watch it grow harder and bigger. I trailed my fingers down his belly until I reached the waistband of his jeans. He was already hard, bulging against his zipper.

He was big. Way bigger than any guy I'd slept with before.

"It'll fit," he said in a heated whisper in my ear. "I'll make sure you're so wet, so open, that you'll be begging me to pound my cock into you." His Irish brogue lengthened with every lewd word. "I'll fill you so full, baby. You'll feel me in every inch of your body."

"I wasn't worried." I smiled deviously as I reached inside his briefs. "But I wanted to inspect the goods first. You know, to make sure you hadn't stuffed a sock in here."

He grunted out a laugh. "Fucking brat." The laugh turned to a groan when I squeezed him. "How about you take me all the way out and see for yourself?"

I could already feel how big he was. He'd fit, but he'd stretch me to my limits. Just the thought of him inside me made my pussy flood.

His cock, roped with veins, his foreskin already pulled back to reveal pre-come on the tip, was magnificent. Of course, I'd never tell him as much. His head was big enough already.

I stroked him from root to tip. I could barely encircle him with one hand.

I kneeled in front of him, breathing hard. Looking up at him through my lashes, I admitted, "I've never done this before."

Liam dug his fingers into my hair. "You don't have to do it now. It can wait."

"No, I want to. Show me what you like."

He gently pushed me toward his cock as he said, "Suck me

inside your mouth. No teeth, mind you. I don't want to end up in the hospital."

I laughed. "You mean blowing a guy isn't like eating corn on the cob?"

"Christ Jesus, woman. Don't even joke about such things."

I swirled my tongue around the tip of his cock like he'd done to my nipples. The salty taste of him made heat bloom in the pit of my stomach.

"Squeeze me as you suck me," he instructed. "Harder. You can't hurt me. As long as you keep your teeth to yourself."

He didn't push me, despite his hand in my hair. I licked and sucked and swirled, moving my hand up and down his length. He somehow grew even harder. The thought that I was driving this man crazy only ratcheted my desire higher.

"Can you take more of me?" he said, pushing my hair away from my face.

I'd never been one to back down from a challenge. "Like deep throat you?"

"We'll see how you do. You're still new for that. But do you trust me?"

I nodded. Because I did—I trusted him implicitly.

"Breathe through your nose. If you need me to stop, pinch me. Now, open your mouth."

He slowly began to feed his cock into my mouth, his hand pushing my head toward his crotch. With every inch, I was certain I couldn't take anymore, but I wasn't one to give up so easily.

"Remember to breathe, baby. Through your nose. God, look at you, with your mouth full of my cock. You're so beautiful."

When he hit the back of my throat, I gagged. Liam pulled free before I'd even pinched him.

"You okay?"

I scowled up at him. "Why'd you stop?"

"You wanna try again?"

"If I want you to stop, I'll tell you. Do it again."

He chuckled, but it turned into a low groan when he pushed inside my mouth again. When he hit the back of my throat, I forced myself to keep breathing through my nose. He held me there for a long moment before gently fucking my mouth and throat.

It was heady, having a man like this use me for his own pleasure. I would've thought it would be demeaning, but it was powerful. I felt powerful even as I was on my knees in front of him.

Liam swore, gripping my hair tightly. I felt his semen hot against my tongue. But before he came, he pulled out, his cock glistening with saliva.

"Fuck, that was amazing. You did so well." He helped me stand. He kissed me, murmuring words of gratitude and praise. "Nothing hotter than seeing you like that, your mouth full of my cock."

"I liked it," I admitted, a little surprised at myself.

Since when was I this sex kitten who loved giving blowjobs? Next I'd be begging to do anal or having Liam tie me up in some *Fifty Shades of Grey* reenactment. I was at the point that if he showed me his red room I'd be totally gung-ho for some spanking.

I remembered all the sexy toys I'd gotten at Jenna's bachelorette party. Maybe I should get the butt plug and put it to good use for once…

"I love that you've only had *my* cock in your mouth," said Liam, his mouth sliding down my throat. "Now take off those jeans and panties before I rip them off."

"You can't rip denim. Not with your bare hands."

When Liam batted my hands away from my jeans and was about to, in fact, actually rip my jeans off, I squealed. "Don't you dare! These jeans cost three hundred dollars!"

"Who spends that much on jeans?" Liam looked at the label. "Are they made with spun gold?"

"They'd be way more than three hundred if that were the case."

Liam wrapped his arm around my waist. "Get your clothes off, wife. Unless you want me to put you over my knee like the bad girl you are."

I was rather tempted by his threat, but perhaps we could save the spanking for another day. Shimmying out of my jeans and panties, I found myself feeling self-conscious for the first time.

I was thin—too thin, honestly. My breasts were small; I was ridiculously pale. Thankfully, I'd shaved all the necessary places this morning, as if I'd intuitively known what was going to happen.

"*Leanan sídhe*," rumbled Liam as he stroked a hand down my side. "Come to suck my very soul from my body."

"What a terrible thing to say."

"It's true. Now get on the bed and spread your legs for me."

I flushed scarlet. I flushed even more when I did as he said, watching him take off the rest of his clothes as he stared down at me. His cock bobbed, still glistening from my mouth. Liam stroked it as he stood at the foot of the bed.

"Spread your legs further. Show me that pussy, wet only for me."

I swallowed and slowly opened my legs. I'd never felt so exposed, so open. My arousal increased until it felt like I had a fever in my blood. I needed him inside me, to fill the empty parts that craved him with every fiber of my being.

Mostly, I just wanted him to fuck me into oblivion.

"There you are," he crooned. "Look how pretty you are. So pink, so wet. God, I've dreamt of that pussy for three days now, my mouth on it, lapping up your juices when you came for me."

I groaned. "Liam…"

"I know." He crawled on top of me, his gaze dark and intense. "Tell me you want me. How you need my cock in that tight pussy of yours."

"I need it," I whispered at the same time he fitted the head of his cock at my entrance. My toes curled in the sheets. "I need you."

Liam's arms bracketed my head as he penetrated me. I could barely breathe. Grasping at his shoulders, I felt full to the brim. Too full, almost. It was pleasure bordering on exquisite pain.

When he was fully seated inside me, his balls resting against my ass, he kissed me. His tongue plunged into my mouth as he began to move.

I saw stars on the backs of my eyelids. I lifted my hips with each of his strokes, desperate for him. As our lips met, so our bodies met and combined into one. He increased his rhythm until the bed squeaked and rocked. He pounded into me relentlessly.

Soon, he lifted my legs and hooked them over his arms, opening me completely. I writhed.

"Liam," I whined. "Don't stop. Please don't stop. I'm so close."

"*A ghrá geal,* I'll never stop." He said something else that I assumed was Gaelic, but he could've been speaking Mandarin for all I cared. I was only sensation; only my stuffed pussy and straining clit. Only sweat and lips and heat and an orgasm pulling tighter and tighter inside me.

"Come for me. Let me feel that pussy come on my cock."

I opened my eyes, my vision hazy, right at the same moment as my release hit me. I arched and screamed. I vaguely heard Liam swear as he thrust three more times inside me before pulling free. Then warm semen splashed against my belly and my breasts.

Liam collapsed beside me. We were both sweat-slicked, panting. I touched a finger to a bead of his come on my belly. I'd never had a man come on me like he just did. It was surprisingly hot, despite the mess.

As Liam went to get cleaned up, I had the stray thought we should've used a condom, but I appreciated that he'd pulled out. Then again, if he was clean it wouldn't matter. I was on birth control. Had been since I'd started dating David.

He's not your husband. Don't expect him to be faithful. Besides, this is temporary, remember?

I knew that, but somehow the idea didn't register in my dopamine-soaked brain. Especially when Liam returned and began to gently wipe me off.

"You good?" His words were gruff, almost awkward.

I yawned. "Get back into bed so we can spoon."

"Yes, wife." He tossed the washcloth onto the bedside table.

Before I fell asleep, I said, "I forgot to tell you: we're having dinner with my family tonight."

Sex must've turned Liam's brain to mush, because he didn't even protest. He just said "Yes, wife," a second time and pulled me into his arms a few seconds before we both fell asleep.

CHAPTER SEVENTEEN

LIAM

Who would have known my prissy little wife was insatiable in bed? After we'd slept for a few hours, I awoke at the same time that she'd turned back toward me, palmed my cock, and had got me hard again like I was some teenager with his first girl.

The fact that Mari's piece of shite ex hadn't so much as eaten her out made me want to prove to her that she was better off with me.

Okay, fine—I didn't want to examine too closely why it mattered. This was just a fling. Hot sex never lasted. It wore off; the luster turned dull. I had no expectations that this was anything more than what I always did with women.

But I'd be a liar if I said I didn't want it to last longer than these six months. That after Mari had fallen asleep, her hair strewn across her pillow, I'd imagined what it'd be like for us to be truly man and wife.

That night, Mari turned to me after I'd parked the car to say, "Are you nervous?"

I shot her an ironic glance. "Should I be?"

"If you're not, I am. My family is…a lot."

"You met my sister. She's basically ten people in one."

Mari laughed. Tonight she'd put her red hair up in some braided thing that made her look like some dairymaid that needed a good tumble on a hill. It didn't help that she wore a white sweater dress, or that she'd worn red lipstick. It took all of my self-control not to take her in the backseat of my car outside her family's house.

"Your sister is just one person. This is five people."

I heard a door swing open, and out came who I assumed was one of Mari's sisters.

"Then we better go into the lion's den before they eat us."

I'd told myself meeting her family was just part of this charade. In their eyes, we were truly married, so why wouldn't they meet me?

Except as I shook hands with her dad and he gave me a look that pretty much said, *I'll take you out back and shoot you if you fuck around*, I found myself wanting to prove him wrong.

"Oh, he's so tall," said Kate, the youngest sister. She wasn't much older than Niamh, although she was taller than my sister. "He's got a jaw you could cut yourself on, too."

"Kate," admonished Mari.

I chuckled. "Thanks for the compliment."

Kate dimpled, but anyone with half a brain cell could tell she had some evil sparkle in her eye. "How drunk were you two when you decided to get married?"

Everyone sighed.

"*Kate*," said Mrs. Wright. "Don't terrorize our guest."

"It's an honest question."

"That doesn't mean you have to say it out loud," said Mari.

Thankfully I was saved from further inquiry when Mrs. Wright basically dragged Kate into the kitchen to help her. Mari took my arm as we went into the living room.

"Sorry about that. Kate likes to rile people," said Mari quietly.

I shrugged. "You remember my sister, don't you? Your sister doesn't scare me."

"You say that, until she puts frogs in your bed." Mari's tone was dark.

Soon I found myself sitting next to the middle sister— Dandelion. Mari had yet to explain why she and Dani were named after flowers but Kate wasn't. Then again, based on the plants hanging in every corner of the room, along with seedlings placed on window ledges, the Wright family didn't do normal or logical.

Dani didn't look anything like Mari. Where Mari was tall and slim, Dani was short and curvy. They didn't even have similar hair or eye colors. I almost wondered if Mari was adopted. Or maybe Mrs. Wright had had a torrid affair with the milkman.

Next to Dani was her fiancé, Jacob, who kept looking at me with a bland expression.

He's the one to watch out for, I thought grimly. *No matter if he makes fucking bouquets for a living.*

Mr. Wright settled in an oversized chair across from the rest of us. He wasn't intimidating to me: he was shorter than me, with a bit of a belly along with a nice-sized bald patch on his head. But I could tell he didn't like me.

"How did you and Mari meet? She didn't explain that part," said Mr. Wright.

"Dad, I told you. He's a mutual friend. He's friends with Sam, Jenna's husband," said Mari.

"You told us about the connection. You didn't tell us how you met."

Mari shifted next to me. I took her hand and squeezed it. I cursed inwardly when I remembered her lack of ring. And of course her father noticed. His face creased.

"Why no ring?" he said.

"Everything has been such a whirlwind that we haven't had time," said Mari.

Which was true, for the most part.

"A real man would've picked one out on his own," said Mr. Wright.

"Dad," interjected Dani, "that's silly. You know how picky Mari is. You can't give her clothes or jewelry that she hasn't picked out on her own. It's pointless. Remember when you and Mom bought her all those sweaters in sixth grade and she secretly returned them all later?"

"It's true. Liam is smart, but he doesn't exactly know my taste in jewelry," said Mari.

Except that she'd told me what she wanted last night, hadn't she? I'd made sure to file that detail away in my brain for later.

"Or he doesn't have enough money to buy you one," countered Mr. Wright.

Mari and Dani protested, but I squeezed Mari's hand to silence her.

"I have plenty of money. I'm happy to show you, if you don't believe me."

"You do not have to show my dad your bank statements. This isn't Jane Austen, where we're figuring out settlements and dowries. Good lord," said Mari.

"I want to know if he can support you. That's what parents are supposed to do. And I have a hard time believing any of this was thought of before you two decided to elope like idiots," said Mr. Wright, crossing his arms across his chest.

"I can take care of your daughter. That you don't have to worry about," I said.

I respected that her dad wanted to make sure she was all right, but that didn't mean he could insult me. "Our marriage might have been quick, but that doesn't make it less legitimate."

Mari stared up at me with wide eyes. Right then, I didn't know which were lies and which was the truth. Everything had blurred together, especially after this morning.

"Dinner's ready," said Mrs. Wright. "Come and sit down, everyone."

I wondered if this was what it was like for Anne Boleyn the night before she got her head chopped off: everyone staring at her, wondering what her next move would be. But I wasn't in the Tower.

I was in the Wright house, where books about gardening lined one wall while the other was lined with crystals, some kind of fancy cards, and a bunch of things that made me pretty sure at least one of the Wright women was a witch. I wouldn't have been surprised if a talking black cat emerged to tell us stories right then.

"What's with all of that?" I said to Mari, tilting my head toward the witch bookshelf. "Should I be worried?"

"My mom is super into astrology and crystals. She'll probably give you a reading later."

"That sounds terrifying." I wasn't religious anymore, but I was tempted to do the sign of the cross anyway.

Mari winked. "Don't worry. She's the nicest one of us."

I wasn't sure that was saying much, given the stares I was currently receiving. Dani was the only person besides Mari that didn't look like she either wanted me dismembered or tortured until I broke.

"What do you do for work?" said Mr. Wright from the other end of the table.

"Photography."

Mr. Wright grunted and sawed at his piece of steak until his fork squeaked against his plate. I'd no idea a man who'd worked as a florist for twenty-plus years would be so against his oldest daughter marrying without telling him.

"Not sure how you can make money off of something like that," said Mr. Wright. "Starving artist and all that."

"Dad, you were a professional floral designer," said Mari wryly.

"I owned my own business. That's different."

"Liam owns his own business, too," said Mari.

After that, Mr. Wright decided he'd rather concentrate on his meal than on me. The conversation flowed, with Dani and Jacob telling a story about a recent client who'd stormed into the shop when she'd discovered an insect in her bouquet.

"She was so upset about it I thought her head was going to explode," said Dani. "I told her sometimes that happened. Plants grow outside, and bugs get on them. She didn't believe me. She said I'd done it on purpose."

"Who doesn't plant an aphid or two in someone's bouquet just because?" said Jacob jokingly.

"You should've put a cockroach in there." This was from Kate.

"We're trying to make money, not be shut down," said Dani, rolling her eyes.

Mari shot me an apologetic grimace. *Sorry*, she mouthed.

You can repay me later, I mouthed back.

She blushed, which only gave me a reason to touch her knee under the table. She wore tights under her white sweater dress, but it was a very thin layer that covered her silky skin. Her breath caught when I traced a single finger up, up, up, edging the hem of her dress away from that pussy I'd had my mouth on in the wee hours of the morning.

She covered my hand with hers and pinched me. All while not looking at me.

I smiled and pinched her back. But it wasn't her hand that I pinched: it was the inside of her thigh.

She jumped in surprise, her leg hitting the bottom of the table with a loud thump. Water sloshed from her glass onto the table.

"Good lord, what was that?" said Mrs. Wright from the other end of the table.

Mari was so red that I had to almost stuff my fist into my mouth to keep from guffawing. When she reached over and dug her nails into my thigh—perilously close to my bollocks— I had to bite my knuckle. Mostly so she didn't completely unman me, the harpy.

"Aw, the lovebirds are playing footsie," crooned Kate, her chin in her hands. "You're so adorable."

After dinner, Mrs. Wright took me aside, her wrists jangling from all her bracelets.

"Don't let George upset you. He's all bark and no bite. He's just mad that he paid so much for Mari's wedding to David and look what happened there." She winced. "Oh, I shouldn't have mentioned He Who Should Not Be Named. Especially not to Mari's new husband."

"Did your husband like David that much?"

Mrs. Wright considered the question. "He seemed like a nice young man. Mari loved him, so we loved him. When Mari told us she was calling the wedding off, we couldn't have been more shocked. She never told us exactly what happened, just that they were over."

I looked at her in surprise. Mari had told me the details of her failed engagement, but not her family?

"Come with me. You look like you need a reading, young man."

Mrs. Wright took me to an office that was filled with more plants than I thought possible. She motioned for me to sit; a small table at about knee-level separated us. Mrs. Wright began to take out various things from under the table. Soon the heavy scent of burnt sage filled the room.

"For cleansing," she explained, waving the sage leaf, her eyes closed. "The energy tonight is full of ragged edges. Especially yours."

I didn't bloody know what the hell she meant by that and I wasn't tempted to ask for clarification. Mari had warned me her family was weird. I hadn't realized they were actually loony.

Mrs. Wright inhaled. "I sense that you need to hold some selenite." She reached inside a velvet pouch and handed me a milky clear stone. "Hold it over your heart chakra. It needs to open."

"My heart what?"

"Close your eyes and feel the white light pulsing through you." Mrs. Wright inhaled deeply. "Can't you feel your chakras opening up?"

"Erm, sure."

"Excellent. I can see them opening up right now. What a bright, purple light you have inside you! Oh, and it's taken the form of a…squirrel? I believe that's what I'm seeing."

The thought of a purple squirrel inside me almost broke me. I had to chew on the inside of my cheek to keep from laughing. Or crying. Those were the only two options at this point.

Mrs. Wright opened her eyes and began to shuffle a deck of cards. "What is your question that you would like to ask Spirit?"

"My question?"

"It can't be a yes or no question."

Mrs. Wright seemed so serious despite telling me I had a fucking rodent in my soul or whatever that I forced myself to think of a question.

"What will happen with Mari and me?" I said, instantly cursing myself.

You already know the answer, bloody idiot.

Mrs. Wright hummed under her breath as she shuffled. And shuffled. And then shuffled for so long I almost fell asleep in my chair. When she finally chose a card and flipped it over, it was upside down.

"Oh, dear," she murmured, tapping the card. "Oh, dear."

"What?"

She clucked her tongue. "This is a protection message, since it's upside down." She showed me the front, which was an image of a burning tree and in the corner, it read *regeneration*. "Sometimes you have to let go of things, end things, to let them become new," she said calmly. "What are you holding onto that you should set free?"

An icy claw grabbed my heart and squeezed until I couldn't breathe. And then I was pissed because the entire thing was so stupid.

I'd already known I'd need to let Mari go. I wasn't cut out for commitment. I'd break her heart just like Da had broken Mam's.

I stared at that card until my eyeballs were liable to fall out of their sockets. I shouldn't have let Mari get under my skin like she had. I knew better.

It was the sex talking, I told myself. Once we fucked enough times and boredom set in, letting her go would be as easy as all the other women.

"There you are," said Mari, breaking through the vicious thoughts coursing through me. "Oh, did you give him a reading?"

"Of course I did. He's my son-in-law." Mrs. Wright patted my knee. "I hope you found that helpful."

My voice was strained as I replied, "So helpful. I never would've thought there was a squirrel inside me."

"A squirrel?" said Mari.

"Yes, a purple one. Didn't you know?" said Mrs. Wright.

"Yes, wife," I said wryly, "didn't you know about the squirrel inside me?"

Mari, for her part, kept her expression completely serene.

"No, but it makes sense. Does this mean you have a fascination with nuts now?"

"Only if you have a fascination with my nuts, too," I drawled.

"Excellent." Mrs. Wright clapped her hands together. "Now I really want to roast some chestnuts. Who's with me?"

CHAPTER EIGHTEEN

MARI

The car ride home from my family's house was silent. I tried to get Liam to tell me what he and my mom had talked about, but he just said she'd only read his cards. "A bunch of bollocks," he'd muttered more than once.

Tonight hadn't gone as well as I'd hoped. Despite telling my dad to lay off Liam, he'd been like a dog with a smelly, disgusting bone. While Liam had been with my mom, I'd told my dad to cool it. He'd countered that he'd "cool it" when he'd seen evidence that I hadn't married a hooligan.

"Dad, a hooligan? Seriously? What year is this, 1955?" I'd said in exasperation.

"That was the nicest term I could come up with."

Lucky for me and unluckily for Dani, our dad had decided that he'd wanted to discuss something with Jacob. Apparently both Dani and I had struck out in the dad approval department. It was up to Kate to win that award—God help us all.

By eleven o'clock, I got dressed in my prettiest new lingerie— a ruby red babydoll that I'd bought for my honeymoon, believe it or not—and waited for Liam to come to bed. He often stayed up late to work. Where I was a morning person, he was a night owl. But he usually forced himself to stop work around this time.

When he was still working by eleven-thirty, I put on a robe and went into the living room, one corner of which he'd made into his office of sorts. He wasn't even working: he was sitting in his chair, staring out onto the night skyline.

"Liam? Are you coming to bed?" I said. If I sounded too much like a wife in that moment, I decided not to think about it. I'd be stupid not to admit to myself the lines had blurred like crazy within the past few weeks living with Liam.

Liam glanced at me, like he was surprised I was even in his apartment. "What time is it?"

"Past eleven-thirty." Pushing my hair over my shoulder, I settled down into his lap, letting my robe open. "I was waiting for you."

A flash of desire sparked in his eyes, especially when he got a nice eyeful of my breasts. "Where did you get that?" he rumbled.

"This? Oh, I've had it forever. But I just hadn't worn it for *you* yet."

That made his face crease, and I realized what my statement implied. *I'd worn it for David.* I winced, adding, "Nobody else has seen me in it."

He gently moved me off his lap. "It's fine. Go to bed. I'll be there soon."

Rejection made my cheeks flush. Too afraid to ask why, I did as he asked.

Maybe he's just distracted with something with his work. Maybe he has a headache.

Maybe, maybe, maybe. You'd think I could ask my

husband, but we weren't at that point. Because we'd never get to that point.

I lay awake in bed until my eyelids were too heavy to keep open. I fell asleep alone.

WORK the following morning was hell: first, I didn't put enough water in the coffeepot, and the coffee burned and made the office reek. Then Leslie got on my case for not answering the phone within two rings. By lunch, I was tempted to say I was having uncontrollable diarrhea and needed to go home.

But none of that mattered with Liam's silence hanging over us both. He hadn't even told me goodbye this morning. Even as grumpy as he was in the morning, he always said that when I left. I'd gotten so used to that husbandly gesture that when I hadn't heard it today, I'd almost started crying.

"Too bad I can't drink at work," I said to myself as I made a cup of tea in the break room. I made a point to choose the tea that needed to steep the longest, just to avoid having to go back to my office.

At least when my marriage to Liam ended I'd have the money to do what I loved. I had that consolation.

Five minutes passed, my tea thoroughly steeped, and I took a sip of it right at the same moment that the one person I thought I'd never see again appeared in the break room doorway.

David.

"Mari," he said heavily. "There you are."

I did what any shocked woman would do: I spit my tea all over my ex and the table between us.

I hadn't meant to—I really hadn't. But seeing David's bespectacled face after months of no communication between us, and at my work, no less, well, spitting was inevitable.

I watched in slow motion as my tea splattered David's face and his glasses, along with his stupid, blue-checkered shirt and even his Dockers. He yelped, putting his hands up.

"What the hell!" he screeched.

"Oh my God." I set my tea down and went to grab a bunch of paper towels. "What are you doing here?"

"Why did you spit your tea at me?" David countered, taking the paper towels in a testy motion. He took off his glasses and tried to wipe them clean, but it only smeared the tea all over the lenses.

I covered my mouth, but the laughter burst forth anyway. Then I collapsed into a chair in a fit of giggles. David glared at me and wiped as much tea-saliva from his face and shirt as he could.

"Is this really that funny?" he said.

"Oh yes, and I'm not at all sorry."

David sighed and sat down across from me. "I can't say that I didn't deserve that."

"Why are you here?"

Annoyance filled me. David and I were over. I'd mourned our relationship, our almost-marriage, all of it. But having him appear like this only brought the memories to the surface.

He deserved an entire pot of boiling tea dumped into his lap for what he'd done.

"I wanted to see you, but you wouldn't answer my calls," he said.

"I blocked your number."

"I figured that. And when I went to your apartment, you'd moved. This was the last place I thought I'd look. Well, besides your folks' place, but I didn't think that'd be a smart idea."

I crossed my arms. "Either tell me what you want or leave. I need to get back to work."

I waited for David to speak. He'd never been all that verbose. He tended to be a man of few words, and he never talked about his feelings. The fact that he'd taken the initiative to come to my work like this said a lot.

Not that I cared. He wasn't my concern anymore.

"I wanted to tell you that Samantha and I broke up," he said quietly. "And how sorry I am for what I did."

"For cheating on me with her, you mean."

"Do you have to say it like that?"

I stared at him. "How should I say it? That you had sexual intercourse with a woman who was not me, and we never agreed to have an open relationship? Does that make it sound better?"

"You don't have to be so harsh about it," he mumbled.

More and more I wondered how I'd ever fallen in love with this man. Maybe I'd never fallen in love with David: I'd fallen in love with the idea of him. He represented what I'd thought I'd needed.

Leslie walked past the break room, but she was on her cell phone and didn't notice my visitor. It was enough of a reminder that I didn't have time to listen to my ex-fiancé.

"Look, I don't have time for this," I said.

"I know, I know. You have to get back to work. I do want to explain, though. Me and Samantha really are over."

"Okay. Good for you guys?"

"Look, I'm going about this all wrong. I've wanted to talk to you. To explain. You deserve that much. After we broke up, things were…complicated."

I snorted. "You realize that was your fault, right? Not mine. I didn't cheat."

His cheeks turned red. "Accusations aren't helpful right now."

Where was the kettle of boiling water when a girl needed it? Getting up, I said, "I have to go back to work. Please leave."

He rose from his chair, but he managed to stop me with three words: "Your makeup thing."

"My makeup thing?"

"Yeah, I have it. It's gold? I think it's blush or something. I found it a few weeks ago."

Okay, he'd caught me. "My Pat McGrath palette?" I'd thought I'd lost it, which had pissed me off immensely. That thing had been over a hundred bucks but was one of the best eyeshadow palettes on the market. It was also sold out every-where. It had been a limited edition palette. The few on eBay were upward of a thousand dollars now. I'd checked when I'd realized mine had disappeared into the ether.

"Yeah, sure," said David. "Whatever that is. I wanted to give it back to you."

"Okay…then give it back to me."

David stared at his feet. "I knew you wouldn't see me a second time if I didn't have it. I just wanted to make sure you'd meet with me and really talk."

The little weasel-faced bastard.

"Seriously? You're bribing me? Or blackmailing me, I

guess. You wouldn't give it back to me if I just asked you, would you?" I said.

"I will. I just want to talk first."

The palette wasn't *that* important. It was eyeshadow, for Christ's sake. But the thought that David wouldn't return it to me because he thought I was scared of meeting with him? That was unbearable. I could listen to him ramble for a half hour for that palette—and for my pride.

"Fine. But if you don't bring that palette, you're dead."

"Thanks, Mari. Unblock my number and I'll text you when and where, okay?"

I rolled my eyes, but not before tossing him some of the leftover paper towels. "You have tea on your crotch, by the way."

WHEN I ARRIVED HOME, Liam wasn't there. For some reason, I was almost relieved at his absence. Maybe because he'd see in my face that not only had I seen my ex-fiancé, but I'd agreed to meet with him.

Liam's not your real husband. You don't have anything to apologize for.

Yet why did I feel guilty? Like I'd agreed to an affair or something?

Liam had already thought I'd been cheating on him. Now I was…sort of. Ugh, talk about overly complicated.

David's visit and Liam's absence brought the memories back: my first date with David; first kiss; his marriage proposal. The first date had been awkward, with David attempting to kiss me but missing my lips and instead kissing my jaw.

He'd been a terrible conversationalist. He'd asked me maybe two questions about myself, instead telling me all about his job, his parents, his older brother, until I'd been close to sneaking out through the back of the restaurant.

But he'd won me over by sheer persistence. And he'd been safe: he hadn't pushed me, he hadn't done anything unexpected. Until the whole cheating thing, obviously. He'd been as steady as the tide. I'd fallen in love with him for that very reason.

Yet now I wondered—could that be the sole basis for loving someone? Before, I'd been confident that David was the best choice for a husband. Now, I didn't know what I wanted in a marriage. In a husband, or a lover.

I hadn't known that passion like what I had with Liam existed. I hadn't known a man who'd pushed me, who'd treated me like I was his equal and not someone simply to protect and place on a high shelf like a porcelain doll. I hadn't realized how limiting my relationship with David had been until I'd rushed into marriage with Liam.

Right then I didn't know what compelled me to take my wedding dress out of its garment bag. I hadn't looked at it since before I'd moved in with Liam. I'd considered selling it, but that would mean admitting I'd never get to wear it.

My heart squeezed as I took in the lace detailing, the tiny pearl buttons below the open back. I set it down on the bed and undressed, knowing that it'd be tricky to get the dress on without assistance. But I didn't care.

With some finagling, I was able to get the dress mostly on. A few buttons I couldn't reach, but it didn't matter.

I'd lost a little weight since the whole breakup, and the dress hung loosely around my breasts. *Why are my boobs always the first to go?* I thought dryly.

I put my hair up in a bun and gazed at my reflection in the full-length mirror I'd brought from my apartment.

I didn't hear the front door open. But I didn't need to hear his voice to know that Liam had come home and caught me wearing my wedding dress that I'd bought to marry another man.

CHAPTER NINETEEN

LIAM

"You look beautiful," I said. I came to stand behind her, both of us gazing at her reflection in the mirror.

She did look beautiful, more beautiful than I could've ever imagined. When I stroked a finger down her spine, she shivered. I kissed the side of her neck.

"I can just see you, a trembling, virgin bride on her wedding night," I whispered in her ear. "I start unbuttoning your dress, one by one, revealing your body to me inch by inch."

"Liam—"

"You'd be shivering, blushing, afraid but also curious. Aroused." I bit a cord in her neck, which made her moan. "You'd be wet for me by the time I'd stripped you naked."

Seeing Mari in this wedding dress made me half mad with wanting her. After last night, I'd told myself I should let her go. I'd only break her heart. I didn't need some bloody card reading to remind me of that. Even if a hundred psychics came to tell me that one thing, I wouldn't need to hear it because I already knew it was the truth.

But Jesus Christ, I wanted to prove that stupid card wrong. I wanted to prove old man Gallagher, Da, even Niamh wrong. I wanted to be the man no one—not even myself—thought I could be.

All those thoughts slipped from my mind just as quickly as Mari's buttons slipped through my fingers. She'd missed some, which made her seem human. Vulnerable.

I wanted her so fucking much I was about to burst with it. I'd go insane with wanting her. And the insane thing was that I'd already fucked her. So why did I crave her with this much intensity still?

That didn't mean I couldn't try to remind her that this wasn't going to last. Or was I reminding myself?

"Tell me to leave you alone, and I will." I'd said the words before. This was the first time I wanted her to tell me to let her go, though.

I could see in the mirror that her pupils were dilated. Her nipples were already hard against the silk bodice of her gown.

"Should I want you to leave me alone?" she finally replied, even as I pushed the sleeves of her gown down her arms.

"Yeah, you should."

You should run, Mari. We both should.

"I've always done what I should do, you know. I did the right thing because it was always safer," she said.

I kissed her shoulder, licking at a freckle there. "Am I safe to you, then?"

"Hardly. You're the most dangerous thing I've ever known."

She sounded so…resigned. It made me angry. I had to force myself not to rip that gown right off of her—the gown she'd bought to wear for another man. Intense, fiery jealousy sped through my veins.

She'd agreed to marry that piece of shite. She'd taken his ring. She'd bought this dress, thinking about how she'd get to be his wife in every possible way.

"You want me," I said, almost viciously. I pushed the dress down until it puddled at her feet.

"Do *you* want *me?*" Mari countered.

She looked like a warrior, wearing only her bra and panties, her chin lifted. I turned her head and kissed her until she gasped into my mouth.

I unhooked her bra, her breasts spilling free. I turned her around and leaned down to take one pale pink nipple in my mouth at the same time as I pinched the other.

Mari inhaled sharply. She pressed her hands against my shoulders, like she wanted to push me away. When I increased the pressure of my mouth, she moaned.

"Liam," she said. She tugged on my hair. "Oh my God."

I lifted my mouth away and looked into her glassy green eyes. Then I blew a stream of air on one swollen nipple. She shuddered.

I sucked on her other tit, loving how silky her skin was, how she arched and moaned with every pull of my tongue. I wondered if I could make her come just from playing with her tits.

"Did your fiancé ever touch you like this?" I said, sounding possessive and almost angry. I tugged at her hair. "Did he ever kiss your tits or lick your pussy for hours?"

Mari had flushed to the roots of her hair. "You can't ask me that."

"Why not? I'm your husband, aren't I?"

"I should know everything about you. Every nook, every cranny. Every fold of your pussy, how you like your clit stroked. Do you like it hard or soft? How many fingers can you take inside that tight pussy before you push me away? I know you like one. How about two? Or even three? We both already know that you love my cock."

"Liam—"

"You don't know? Or you won't tell me?" I licked her ear. "I bet you know exactly how many fingers you can fit inside your pretty pussy. You can't tell me you haven't fucked yourself, *a ghrá geal.*"

"I don't like to use my fingers," she admitted. "I just use a vibrator, usually."

"On your clit?"

She licked her lips. "Yes."

I pushed her panties down, exposing her mound. She'd shaved this morning. Her bare pussy made my cock harden painfully.

"Show me," I said. "Show me how you rub your clit, wife."

Mari didn't protest now. She was too desperate to come. When she parted her outer lips, I could see how wet she was already, her clit having already emerged from its hood.

"Show me," I repeated, growling.

She began to lightly tap her clit, her back arching. She slowly increased the pressure as she rubbed that swollen nub.

I couldn't help myself: I took out my aching cock and began to stroke it as she touched herself. Pre-come had already leaked from the head, making it easy for me to glide my hand up and down my shaft.

Mari's eyelids lowered as she watched me.

"Every night since that night in your hotel room," I rasped, "I've thought of your pussy clenching around my finger. How you got my palm so wet. How I could hear how juicy you were as I fucked you, wishing it had been my cock instead of my finger. When you finally let me taste you, it was like tasting heaven and hell at the same time."

Mari's mouth opened wide. "Liam…" she squeaked.

"Are you coming, sweetheart?"

"I'm so close, so close."

She grabbed my arm with one hand, like she was about to lose her balance. Her pussy was totally exposed, completely open to my gaze. It was so lewd and sexy at the same time that it took two more pumps for me to start coming.

My balls drew up before I came on Mari's pussy and fingers. I groaned as I watched her rub my come against her clit. Christ, she was going to fucking kill me.

I reached down and helped her rub that little swollen bud. "Do you know how beautiful you are?" I said in her ear. "Covered in my come as you rub yourself?"

"Liam, Liam." She hung on tightly. Soon she gave into my fingers, as if she knew I'd give her a better orgasm.

That's right, wife. I know how to make you scream.

She came with a shout. She crumpled against me, but I swung her into my arms and carried her to my—our —bedroom.

"You're mine. No matter who you bought that wedding dress for—you're mine," I said.

Her eyes were glassy, her cheeks flushed. She wrapped her arms around my neck and drew me down for a kiss. I kicked her legs open and notched my cock at her tender entrance.

She was still shivering, her pussy contracting so that it was a bit of a struggle to push inside her.

"Liam," she gasped.

"Fuck, you're tight for me, baby." I rammed into her, not caring if I was too hard or too fast. I wanted her with a desperation that scared me. "You still coming for me as I fuck this pussy?"

She couldn't speak. I laughed darkly and pounded into her relentlessly. But I needed more. I needed everything she could give me.

I flipped her over. "Get on your knees," I said.

She did as I said, which said how lost she was in her own desire. Mari in her right mind would've told me to eat shit for being so bossy. I yanked her to the edge of the bed as I stood behind her. I parted her folds, teasing her entrance, loving how pink and swollen she was. She moaned and shimmied her hips.

I didn't give her time to relax, though. I slammed back into her and pounded into her until her moans turned into yells.

I wanted her to unravel. I wanted her to feel how much I was unraveling because of her.

I rubbed her clit in rhythm to my thrusts. "Come for me," I said. "One more time, *a ghrá geal.*"

"I can't. I can't." Her voice was muffled.

"Yeah, you can. You can do anything."

I rubbed her harder. When I felt her clench around my cock, I gave a shout of triumph. She screamed her release at the same time my own release hit me. I poured myself into her until my come overflowed and dripped down her slit.

I could only collapse beside her, utterly spent. We were

both damp with sweat, but I didn't care. I pulled her into my arms and held her until she stopped shivering.

We didn't say anything for a long moment. We didn't need to. I pushed her hair from her face, loving the contrast of the red against her pale skin. Inspiration struck right then.

"Stay here," I said, walking naked into the living room to grab one of my cameras. I fiddled with a few lenses, considering which one would work best for this.

When I returned, Mari hadn't budged. She was lying on her side, one eye open and watching me languidly.

I began to take photos of her, the click of the camera the only sound.

"Oh," said Mari. She pulled the sheets up. "Wait, what are you doing?"

I grinned. "Stay in that pose. Yeah, perfect." I looked at the photo I'd just taken, and I groaned. "Fuck, you're sexy. Lay back down for me."

Mari rolled her eyes, but she didn't protest again. Now that she'd been thoroughly fucked and was in a haze of post-orgasm happiness, she was the perfect model, all ease and sensuality. Each photo I took was better than the last.

I'd told myself Mari wouldn't become my muse. But she'd become my *leanan sídhe,* and I couldn't regret it. Even if she killed me in the end.

"*A ghrá geal,*" I said. "My gorgeous little wife."

After I got back into bed with her, she said, "What does that word mean? You never told me. Not the vampire one. The other one. I tried to look it up, but I have no idea how to spell it."

My heart clenched. *You bloody idiot.*

Thank God for Gaelic's ridiculous spelling rules. I didn't want to explain that one right now.

"It means 'wife,'" I lied.

"Oh. That's not as exciting as I thought it'd mean."

I looked into her eyes and tilted her chin up. "Maybe not, but I mean it. Things have changed between us. And I've been wondering if we shouldn't see where this leads."

My heart pounded so hard I felt sick, especially when Mari said nothing. When she rose from the bed and began to get dressed, I knew I'd misstepped.

Bollocks, bloody, bloody, bollocks.

I'd caught feelings for her, and goddamn it all, she didn't feel the same. I felt instantly like utter shite. What a damn idiot I was.

"You can't tell me you don't feel what's between us," I said in a low voice.

She shrugged "It's just sex."

"It is not just sex. Don't fucking lie to me or to yourself."

She flinched, but being the goddess she was she didn't burst into tears. She just lifted that pointy chin. Staring down at me, her lowly servant in front of his queen, she said, "You were the one who made the deal, Liam. Six months and we were done. Are you reneging?"

I got up from the bed, not caring that I was buck naked. "No, I'm not reneging. I'm changing the terms."

"I have to agree first, you know."

"You're going to stand here and act like you didn't just scream my name as I came inside you? That you didn't try to seduce me last night? You care. I know you care. You're just too scared to admit it because it's easier for you to stay in the bubble you've created."

"You have no idea what you're talking about."

"No? You almost married a man who you didn't even like sleeping with. You stay at a job you don't like when you know you could do something else. You'd rather be miserable and safe than take a risk and be happy for once. Just admit it: you're a coward."

She paled. "Now you're just being deliberately cruel."

Her voice wavered, but she didn't back down, either. She just walked out of my bedroom without another word.

TWO DAYS LATER, I knew I'd fucked up badly. Mari wouldn't speak to me. She wouldn't let me touch her. She just looked at me like I'd tried to drown a sack of puppies in front of her.

I'd never had anyone look at me like that: with disappointment that I existed.

Well, except for old man Gallagher. But I didn't give a shite what he thought about me.

"Let's try smiling without teeth," I said to the couple I was taking photos of at a park in the city. The guy was one of those people who look constipated every time he smiled for a photo. Flipping through the ones I'd taken already, I knew it'd be a struggle to find a decent one.

The guy smiled without teeth, but he widened his eyes so he looked like a serial killer. Fucking hell.

His fiancée looked up at him and scowled. "Why are you making that face?"

"I'm not making a face," he countered.

"These pictures are supposed to be romantic. Why aren't you taking them seriously?"

"Like you took my knitting class seriously? You laughed when I gave you that scarf for your birthday."

"Because it was ugly!"

The bickering only continued, like I didn't even exist. Whatever. They were still paying me by the hour. If they wanted to fight about knitting, that was their problem, not mine.

"Do you even love me, Phil? Do you? Because there are times I'm not sure you do."

"I bought you a ring, didn't I? I think that's a sign that I love you."

"It was only three carats. Three. Carats. And it wasn't even a diamond. You know I didn't want a sapphire!"

I sat down on a bench and began to go through my phone. I'd texted Mari this morning, telling her we needed to talk, but she hadn't responded. But there was a *Read at 10:32 AM* receipt below the message. Great. My own wife refused to answer my texts.

When the bickering turned into a tousle—mostly the woman pushing at her fiancé's arm and him rolling his eyes— I decided I'd had enough. I put my fingers to my lips and whistled loudly.

The couple stopped.

"Look, you two can kill each other for all I care, but I have work to do. Either you want photos, or you don't. But I'm billing you for this time regardless."

The two considered me. Then each other. Then realizing they were literally wasting money, the guy muttered, "Let's get this done."

Those photos? Suffice to say they were unintentionally the

most hilarious and worst photos I'd ever taken of two people supposedly in love.

That was what love turned into, I reminded myself as I packed up my camera and tripod. I'd gone out on a limb, and had fallen so hard my nose was broken. Hadn't I told myself this would happen? That I had to let Mari go?

I just hadn't realized that it would be Mari rejecting me. I'd always been the one to turn women down. Yeah, it hurt my pride, but it hurt the thing inside me that resembled a heart even more.

Was this love? Because if it was, it was bullshite. I'd be better off alone than dealing with this.

It wasn't like I'd got a great example of love with my parents. Da had given up everything for Mam, and then he'd turned around and left us all to starve. If love existed, it never lasted. It was better to end things now.

I told myself that, but it didn't make me feel better.

Walking to my car with heavy steps, I watched a man sit down next to a woman on a bench a few yards away. The woman had bright red hair like Mari's.

When the woman turned so I could see her profile, I realized it *was* Mari. And that man? He was holding her hand—like he had a right to touch her.

But when that man leaned over and kissed her?

I didn't think. I only reacted as red filled my vision.

There are many things in my life that I never expected to happen. Including my almost-husband and my current husband battling it out in the middle of a park like two of the biggest idiots in existence.

My morning had started peaceful enough. I'd bought coffee and sat down to wait for David to show up. I'd considered bailing at least five times, though, but the lure of getting my favorite eyeshadow palette back was too much to give up.

Besides, if David wanted to grovel and apologize some more, who was I to stop him? It wasn't like he'd convince me to get back together with him.

David showed up ten minutes late. "Were you waiting long?" he said.

I sipped my coffee. "Long enough."

He grimaced. "Sorry. Got up late. I'm glad you agreed to meet me, though." He took in my appearance—old jeans, no makeup, my hair in a messy bun—and said, "You look beautiful."

I glared at him. "I'm not here for compliments."

"I know. But I'm here to give them to you. Or at least tell you why I fucked up so badly." He sighed. "You're still angry, I know, but I realized that I'd made a huge mistake. Samantha —she was never anything to me. She was just a distraction."

"I'm not really interested in hearing about her."

"I know, I know. I'm doing this all wrong." David pushed his fingers through his hair. "I was never good at words. You know that."

"You seem to have enough of them right now."

He looked at me with narrowed eyes. "Since when did you get so cynical?"

Excellent question. Or maybe the true question was: why had I been so naive before?

"In case you haven't noticed," I said with a sigh, "I've had to grow up since you dumped me and canceled our wedding. Time passed for me just like it did for you."

"Of course it did. I know that." David went silent for a long moment. "I'm not trying to justify what I did. It was wrong. I made the choice, and I realized only later that I destroyed the best thing in my life. You were the greatest thing I had in my life, and I was an idiot to let you go."

David reached over to take my hand, but I wouldn't let him. Good lord, I did not have time for this.

"What are you saying?"

He leaned closer to me. "I want you back, Mari. I love you."

Those words were an arrow to my heart, but not because of who had said them. Liam had tried to say last night— what? That he loved me? No, he didn't love me. He was blinded by amazing sex. He'd thank me later.

We'd made a plan, and we'd stick to that plan. I already

knew what happened when I let myself love a man: I got hurt. Things ended. If I could thank David for anything, it was showing me that bit of harsh life advice.

I sighed, returning to the task at hand.

"I appreciate the apology, but it's over. You ended it, and you betrayed me, David. That's not something I'm going to ever forget. I might forgive, but I can't trust you again."

My mind went back to those dark days after I'd found out about David's betrayal. That old familiar anger bubbled inside me and kept me from feeling sorry for him.

I continued, "Not only did you cheat on me, but you made me have to tell our friends and family that our wedding was off. Do you know how humiliating that was? To get the phone calls and texts that tried to sound supportive but were just full of pity?" My voice hardened with each word. "Do you know that my grandmother called to give me advice on how to get you back. 'Did you nag him too much, my dear? Men don't like that. I'm not surprised he strayed.'"

"I take responsibility for my actions," he said, his forehead creased, "but you can't say that you had absolutely nothing to do with it, either. You were never the warmest person. Sometimes I wondered if I ever really knew you, or if you even liked me."

A brutal niggle of self-doubt bit me right in the heart, damn him. Had I driven him to another woman's arms without realizing it? Was Liam right—I was too much of a coward to take a risk and thus drove people away? God, I wanted to throw up.

"I don't think I knew you either," I said quietly.

"Then why be upset? According to you, we were better off apart."

That tiny voice went up in a puff of smoke, transformed into a cold anger. Taking a deep breath, I stabbed the knife further into David's heart. He'd already done it to me—I could at least return the courtesy. I wasn't Mari with her head in the clouds anymore. I was cynical, and I was ruthless.

"I'm already with someone else."

I'd rejected that someone else last night, but David didn't need to know that.

David's face paled. He was already pale, but this made him look like he was going to faint. The thought of my ex swooning at my feet was enough to make me start laughing hysterically.

"Who is it? Do I know him?" he said.

"Probably not."

I expected David to slink away, tail between his legs. To my shock, he took my hand and wouldn't let it go.

"I love you, Mari. I screwed up, but I'm willing to fight to get you back. You're the only woman I'll ever love."

His grip was surprisingly firm. "Maybe you should've thought about that before you had sex with another woman *in our bed*."

"I know. I know, you're right. I'm sorry. What can I do to get you to take me back?"

"You're assuming I want you back."

"Just give me a chance to explain. That's it. You don't have to make a decision one way or the other right this second. But at least consider it. Please?"

But then David leaned over and kissed me, the jerk. Before I could react, Liam suddenly appeared like a bat out of hell. If a bat were over six feet tall of rugged, pissed-off Irishman.

And then before I knew it, Liam had tackled David and they were battling it out right in front of me.

"Battling" was a bit of a misnomer, however. David was currently on the ground while Liam swore something in Gaelic that probably amounted to *I'm gonna kill you, you little shite* as Liam pummeled him. I wasn't on the up and up with murderous Gaelic statements, however. Maybe it was more like, *let's go drink some beer down at the pub after this.*

A man came up to me. "Are they fighting?" He was wearing running gear and was slick with sweat. He was running in place as he watched Liam push David's face into the grass. "Or are they just wrestling?"

"I think they're fighting," I said. "It's just that one of them doesn't know how."

"Should we call the police?"

I tilted my head to the side and sighed when David managed to hit Liam on the jaw.

"No. I'll take care of these two."

Before sitting down on this bench to wait for David, I'd bought a large coffee that I'd barely touched. So, luckily for me, I had that at my disposal to dump on two of the stupidest human beings in existence.

The coffee had cooled, but it was enough that Liam sputtered and David had a chance to scramble away. He was covered in grass stains, his glasses askew. Liam, for his part, looked barely rumpled.

"Jesus Christ, what the hell?" said Liam as he stood up, coffee staining his shirt. "The bloody hell did you do that for?" His Irish accent had emerged to the full degree, and if I weren't so pissed at him, I would've found it sexy.

"What the hell am I doing? What the hell are *you* doing? You can't just attack people in the middle of a park!"

"I can when they're pawing at my wife!"

David kept looking back and forth between us. When Liam said *wife*, David's mouth dropped open. "You're married?"

Liam sneered. "She neglected to tell you that, did she?"

"Oh my God." I turned to David and said, "Will you get out of here? Wait—give me my palette."

David looked like he had no idea what I was talking about. Finally, he muttered something under his breath, tossed me my palette, and took off jogging. I'd never seen David move that quickly before.

Liam swiped his hand over his face. "What the fuck was that? Why did you agree to meet with that rat bastard?"

"If you'd stop yelling at me, I'd tell you."

"You seriously go from my bed last night to another man's this morning?"

"We're in a public park, not a hotel!"

Liam pulled me into his arms, his breath hot against my face.

"You're married to me. Did you forget me stripping you out of your wedding gown and fucking you like a good little wife last night? I was the one who made you scream, not him."

I gaped up at him. "Are you serious right now?"

"Do I look like I'm joking?"

We stared each other down, both of us breathing hard. I didn't care that passersby were pointing at us, whispering under their breaths about the drama unfolding in the middle of the park.

"Why did you come here to meet him?" Liam dug his fingers into my upper arms. "Why, Mari?"

It was so stupid now, coming here for a bit of eyeshadow, but I had a feeling that hadn't been why I'd agreed. Because I'd wanted David to beg? Because Liam had tried to make me think we could make this real and I'd known better? But Liam's anger, his impulsiveness, just served to remind me that any relationship we'd have would be messy and unpredictable. And then when Liam got bored, then what?

I'd be alone again. I'd be the girl left to pick up the pieces, just like with my mom and with David.

I pulled myself from his arms. "You don't control me. This isn't real! It never has been!"

"You're lying to yourself and to me. Tell me you don't love me."

I stared at him in shock. I was about to deny my feelings, but it was then that I realized I did love him.

I loved him, and I knew I could never have him.

Losing David had been shitty. Losing Liam? That would be brutal. I felt my heart already breaking inside me.

"You can't answer me." Liam looked triumphant. "Because you care more than you'll admit."

"Have you listened to what you're saying? First I'm getting back with my ex, now I'm in love with you. Which is it? Because clearly I don't know, either."

"Because you don't know what you want. And I bet you're so afraid of feeling something for me you thought you could make yourself feel better by seeing the man who never demanded anything of you."

Liam forced me to look into his eyes. "You care," he said quietly. "I can see it in your eyes. But you won't take the risk."

All I had now was my tattered pride. I pulled it around myself like a mantle. "You don't know a damn thing about me. Now let me go."

Liam's expression hardened. "Such an ice queen. No wonder David cheated on you, with a woman that cold in his bed."

I slapped him. I'd never slapped anyone in my entire life. Not even David, even though he'd deserved it.

"This is over," I said. "I want a divorce."

I didn't let the tears fall until I got inside my car. Then I leaned my forehead against the steering wheel and sobbed.

CHAPTER TWENTY-ONE

MARI

You'd think by now I'd know what to do after a breakup. Buy some Ben and Jerry's, watch sad movies, cry a while. Feel sorry for myself, definitely. I'd done all of that after I'd found out David was cheating on me.

But this? This was a million times worse. This felt like my entire heart had been ripped out, stomped on, and thrown to the crows to eat.

Worst of all, the world kept turning. I still had to go to work. I still had to act like I wasn't completely dead inside, because then I'd have to admit to everyone how much I still loved my husband. Yet I was so angry with him that I wasn't sure if I'd slap him or hug him if I saw him again.

At the moment, I was staying with Dani and Jacob. When I'd shown up at their door that afternoon after my epic fight with Liam, bags in hand and sobbing, Dani hadn't asked any questions. She'd bustled me inside, made me a cup of tea with a large shot of either brandy or whiskey, and had let me tell my story when I'd been ready.

"Have you heard anything from him?" said Dani. It was

two weeks after my breakup, and Dani had somehow persuaded me to go out with her and Kate for dinner.

I stared at my gin and tonic, swirling the ice around the glass.

"No. And I haven't contacted him except to ask him to let me into the apartment so I could get most of my stuff."

"But he hasn't filed for divorce?" said Dani.

"Not that I'm aware of." I'd been meaning to talk to a lawyer, but every time I'd picked up my phone to call the one Jacob had recommended, I'd hesitated. I told myself I didn't have the emotional strength to deal with that right this second.

"So you're just going to stay married to him forever?" said Kate, in that voice that said *that's the stupidest thing I've ever heard.* "At least if you divorce, you'll get money out of him."

"That was the deal, actually. We'd stay married until his sister got her inheritance. Now…" I shrugged. "I don't know what'll happen."

"You can't just let this go on indefinitely," said Dani.

"Sure, I can. I'll just ignore it," I joked, but it fell flat, like a dead fish tossed onto the table.

Did I feel guilty that I'd potentially screwed Niamh out of her inheritance? Yes, and no. Liam wasn't innocent in all of this, either.

Kate and Dani looked at each other. Something passed between my two younger sisters. Normally, as the oldest, I'd demand to know what it was, but I didn't want to know.

In all of this, I discovered that sometimes it was simply easier to remain ignorant. Ignorance hurt less.

Dani cleared her throat. "Mari, I actually asked you out because we need to be honest with you. I'm happy to let you stay at my place for however long you want, but watching you just suffer and not try to move forward—"

"It's dumb," interjected Kate.

I barely reacted to Kate's words. I didn't care that it was dumb. What did it matter?

"It's not dumb, but it isn't like you, either," said Dani, shooting a glare at Kate. "You aren't the type to sit passively by. Either you're getting a divorce or you're going to fix your marriage. You can't just let this sit and rot."

The first stirrings of anger since that day in the park bloomed inside me. "How would you even know?" I countered, looking at both of my sisters. "You have no idea what I've gone through."

"We would if you'd tell us," said Kate under her breath.

Hadn't I already told them all about my Vegas wedding, my bargain with Liam? I hadn't kept anything from them. They knew the entire sordid tale by now.

"It's just that this whole thing…" Dani sighed. "You aren't acting like the Mari we know. That's all. And we hate to see you so sad and brokenhearted. Don't you want to pick up the pieces?"

"It's been two weeks," I said.

"Long enough to know what your next move will be."

I'd just picked up my drink, and I found myself slamming it back onto the table in frustration. Both Dani and Kate jumped.

It was as if a dam had burst. A river overflowing. A cup overturned. Whatever water metaphor suited your fancy.

"You don't have any idea, do you? Because I've always been the one protecting you two," I said.

My sisters looked gobsmacked. Kate had a French fry halfway to her mouth as she stared at me.

"What are you talking about?" said Dani.

I let out a breath. "When Mom left, I kept that from you two because I was the oldest. To you guys, things have always been safe and secure. I know better. I know that there is no such thing."

I swallowed, a lump in my throat. "And Liam? He just proved it to me a hundred times over. So, no, I'm not doing anything because, to me, it seems pointless to keep this charade going. What's the point of giving your heart away when your mom, your ex-boyfriend, and then your husband just end up leaving you?"

Both Dani and Kate stared at me like I'd sprouted horns. Then Kate blurted, "Mom *left*? When? For how long?"

Dani was white. "Did Mom and Dad almost get divorced?"

I sighed, realizing I'd have to explain myself now. I told them both of Mom leaving, and how I'd been the one to take care of them both. Kate had only been a baby, but Dani's eyes widened as she realized that those two weeks when Mom had been gone had been for an entirely different reason.

"Why did you keep that to yourself?" said Dani. Her eyes were shining with tears. "You shouldn't have kept that burden."

Kate had crossed her arms over her chest, saying nothing. That was a first. But it didn't last long.

"So let me get this straight," said Kate. She had her fork in her hand, and she pointed it toward me. "Because other people have fucked up around you, you believe it's because you're unlovable and that people will always leave? That makes zero sense."

I blushed. "It's more complicated than that."

"Doesn't sound like it."

"I don't really need my teenage sister lecturing me," I shot back.

"Maybe you do, because obviously I'm the smartest one here. Look, you can wallow and be a big dingus-face if you want, but then you'll be unhappy forever and I'd hate that because I'd never want to be around you again. Put on your big girl panties, Mari. Life is scary and sometimes you need to take a risk. And yeah, sometimes people leave. But Mom came back, didn't she?"

Both Dani and I were staring at our little sister. Then Dani started laughing, breaking the tension.

"What's so funny?" I muttered.

"I don't know. Everything. Nothing. The fact that our baby sister is so wise now. But then in an hour she'll probably do something stupid and everything will return to normal," said Dani.

Kate snorted. "That's just uncalled for."

"Didn't you tell me that you got caught sneaking a goose into your dorm room to prank your roommate?" said Dani.

"Oh no, we didn't get caught until after Bethany had screamed when she'd found the goose." Kate grinned evilly. "That's what happens when you take credit for a project you didn't do any work for."

"Poor girl," I said, but Kate just shrugged. More than likely, this Bethany probably deserved the goose invasion.

Most of all, I wanted to continue to stew in my own hurt. I wanted to wallow. I wanted to make myself the victim.

But that was easy, wasn't it?

"I'm still in love with him," I moaned, covering my face with my hands.

"Well, duh. Everyone knows that," said Kate.

"What Liam said to you was uncalled for. You have every right to be angry with him."

Dani took my hands away from my face so I had to look her in the eye.

"I was the same with Jacob. He hurt me badly. I thought it was over, even though my feelings hadn't changed one bit. But when he realized he'd lost me, he gave up something important to show me how much I mattered to him."

"What's your point?" I said, wary.

"Just that for love, sacrifices are necessary. And it's the one thing worth sacrificing for. That's all."

"What Dani is saying," said Kate as she tossed an olive from Dani's plate into her mouth, "is that some major groveling needs to happen pronto."

"I don't think groveling is going to convince Liam that he's actually in love with me," I said in a small voice.

"Won't know until you try." Kate grinned. "So how about you get out there and show us how it's done, big sister?"

THE FOLLOWING DAY, I went to my parents' house. I didn't know if my mom would offer any answers, but I needed to ask anyway.

I needed to understand why she'd left, because I'd realized, after dinner with my sisters, that I'd held in that pain for so long that it had made me believe there was something wrong with me.

"Mari, sweetheart! This is a nice surprise." My mom hugged me, smelling of lemon and patchouli. "Your dad is at the store. Something about a hydrangea crisis. I didn't ask. I told him that he's retired, but he gets bored around the house. He never was a golfer, you know."

My mom always seemed so *happy*, so normal. What had pushed her to leave her daughters and husband all those years ago?

"Mom," I said quietly, "I need to tell you something. About Liam and I, and…other things."

The one thing good about my mom was that she was good at listening until you finished speaking. She didn't interrupt as my story poured from me. I told her about Vegas, about Niamh, about falling in love with Liam. About how it had ended, which I hadn't been comfortable explaining two weeks ago.

"I'm sorry I didn't tell you and Dad sooner. I just—didn't know how. It was such a ridiculous situation. You guys were already skeptical about our marriage. Telling you that it wasn't real?" I shuddered. "Dad would've had a stroke."

"Well, I have to admit, I didn't expect you to do something like that," said my mom. "Kate? Yes. Dani? Maybe, only because she was too oblivious to realize what she'd gotten herself into. But you were always so responsible. Look at David: he was the most responsible choice. Until he went off the deep end."

"There's another reason why I wanted to talk to you." I took a deep breath, my palms sweaty. "I know about you leaving us. When I was eight."

My mom's smile died on her face. I felt guilty bringing it up, but it had lain dormant for too long.

"I never left you guys," she said quietly. "Not really."

"That's what Dad said. He didn't know if you were coming back, though." I swallowed against the lump in my throat. "I used to lay awake at night, terrified I'd never see you again."

"Oh, sweetheart." My mom took my hand and squeezed it. "There was no doubt in my mind I'd return. Your dad should've made that clear. I thought all this time you thought it was a business trip. That's why I've never mentioned it. To protect you and your sisters."

"Why did you leave then?"

My mom sighed, gazing off into the distance.

"You have to understand—I wasn't myself back then. Kate was a surprise pregnancy, and she wasn't an easy birth. Then afterwards, I was hit really hard with postpartum. But I didn't know that was what it was. I had three girls to take care of, plus the store. Your dad did his best, but when your brain is sick, there's nothing anyone can do to cure that, you know?"

I stared at her, stunned. I'd had no idea. "Did Dad know?"

"Yes and no. He knew, but he didn't want to believe I was that depressed. It didn't help that I didn't talk about it. It was a big mess, sweetheart. And when I left, it was because I was afraid of myself." My mom looked stricken. "I knew I had to get help before I could come back. I left for all of you."

"Where did you go?"

"I checked into a psych ward," she said bluntly. "Two weeks isn't long enough to cure depression like that, but it stabilized me. Enough that I could come back home and do outpatient treatment."

At this point, we were both crying.

"I thought I'd done something wrong. And I was so afraid to ask," I said.

"Mari, no. I love you. You were a little girl. It wasn't anyone's fault." My mom pulled me into a hug. "I should've told you sooner. If I'd known you thought that…"

I cried on her shoulder, letting the tears that I'd needed to shed flow. Tears for me as a little girl; tears for my marriage that seemed destined to never recover. Tears for loving a man who thought I was too cold, too afraid to love.

"I was afraid there was something wrong with me. You, then David, then Liam," I whispered.

"The only thing wrong with you is you thinking that. And if Liam is as smart as I think he is, he'll realize what he's lost. Just like you have, if I'm correct. If you two love each other, you'll find a way back to each other."

My mom smiled, her eyes wet. "Just invite me to the wedding next time, will you?"

CHAPTER TWENTY-TWO

LIAM

When the prints of the photos I'd taken of Mari arrived, I didn't look at them for days.

I'd ordered them before that fight in the park. After our disagreement that night, though, I shouldn't have tweaked fate's nose. But I'd been hopeful. And fucking stupid.

I grabbed a glass of whiskey and, sitting on the couch that somehow still smelled like my wife, I opened the package.

I thumbed through the photos: one of Mari smiling, looking away from me. One of Mari with her eyes closed, a pink nipple just peeking out from below the bedsheet. Mari smiling at me, every emotion under the sun shining from her face.

But I'd told her that I loved her and she hadn't told me the same. And then I'd said those words I wished I could take back. And now our marriage was over, and all that work I'd put in to keep Niamh's inheritance intact? Down the drain, as soon as old man Gallagher caught wind of things.

Lucky for me, though, that Mari had yet to file for divorce.

I didn't know what she was waiting for. Maybe she just wanted me to stew as I waited for the ax to fall.

I slammed back the rest of the whiskey and went for a refill.

That was how Niamh found me. Half-drunk, morose, and feeling sorry for myself.

"Oh my God, when is the last time you *cleaned?*" Niamh wrinkled her nose when she saw the array of empty bottles and dirty dishes on the coffee table. "This is the saddest thing I've ever seen."

I barely reacted to her entrance. "What are you doing here? Don't tell me you've run away again."

"Of course not." Niamh sat down on the couch, only to scowl when she found dirty socks under the throw pillow. "Aunt Siobhan needed to come to Seattle this weekend. So here I am." Niamh peered at me. "Where's Mari?"

"She left."

"Like, she went out for the night?"

I sighed heavily. "No, Niamh. She left me. We're over."

"Oh." Niamh folded her hands in her lap. "Why are you guys over? I liked her."

"Because I'm bloody moron, that's why. I told her I loved her and wanted to make our marriage a real one—"

"Wait, wait, wait. *Marriage?* You two were married? Since when?"

"Since I went to Vegas and married her when we were both rat-arsed."

Niamh gaped at me, and it would've been funny if I'd been in a laughing mood.

"You guys were married when I was here? But you said

she was your girlfriend! Not your wife. Why wouldn't you have told me that?"

I heard the hurt in her voice, and guilt filled me. I'd fucked everything up with the people I'd loved, hadn't I? I'd hurt Mari; I'd hurt Niamh. And now that my marriage was over, Niamh wouldn't get her inheritance.

"It was complicated," I said. I grimaced when I realized I'd finished my tumbler of whiskey already. "It wasn't worth explaining to you."

"How about you try to explain it to me now. Speak slowly, though. I might not understand if you don't."

"You're a pain in the arse, you know that?"

"Spill your guts already. I'm waiting."

I wasn't about to spill my guts to my little sister without more liquor in me. After refilling my glass, I returned to the couch, almost amused that Niamh was the one acting like the mature, older sibling now. Clearly the universe was upside down at the moment.

I told her the entire story—the wedding, the deal, her inheritance, old man Gallagher. How I'd fallen for my wife and how she'd rejected me without so much as a tear shed. How I'd said those cruel words to her and regretted saying them so much I ached with it.

Unlike Mari, Niamh wasn't one not to interject her opinions throughout your story. But by the time I got to the end, she was out of words. She just gaped at me, her mouth wide open.

"You're going to collect flies in your mouth if you don't close it," I said wryly. I tapped her under her chin. "Nothing to say now?"

Then, to my utter horror, she burst into tears. Noisy,

sobbing tears. I'd never heard my sister cry like that—at least not since she was a small girl.

"Fucking hell," I muttered, "what's the matter? What did I say?"

"You idiot! You giant, dumbass, moronic doofus! You have shit for brains! I could punch you in the face right now!"

"Good lord, it can't be that bad."

Niamh wiped her eyes, but the tears kept flowing.

"You did all of this...*for me*. How could you? I never, ever would've made you agree to that."

Even with the whiskey in my belly, I was able to put two and two together.

"I'd do anything for you. And you deserve to go to the best university you can. I wasn't about to put that in jeopardy because of some stupid, drunken mistake."

"Can't you see, though? If Grandda decided to cut me off because of what you did, that would be on him, not you." Niamh sniffled. "I wouldn't have blamed you. Grandda is totally cuckoo for Cocoa Puffs. Everybody and their dog knows that."

Having your teenage sister talk such obvious sense wasn't exactly great for a guy's ego. I rubbed the back of my neck, wondering if the heat in my cheeks was from the booze or from embarrassment.

"I thought I was doing the right thing," I said finally.

Niamh sighed heavily, then punched me in the bicep. I winced.

"You should've just told me, dumbass."

"Like I said: I thought I was doing the right thing."

We fell into silence, the only sounds from the traffic outside my flat. The sun had long since set, and a sliver of a crescent moon showed in the sky. I wondered if Mari was looking up at the moon right now. Which was so fucking sentimental I wanted to drink until I passed out.

I was about to get another refill when Niamh launched herself into my arms, hugging me so hard the air went out of my lungs for a moment.

"I love you," she said into my neck. "But you don't have to be my knight in shining armor anymore. I'm a big girl now."

I snorted, hugging her back. "You're my little sister. It's my job. When Mam died, I promised her I'd look after you. And I hope I've kept that promise."

Niamh drew back and smiled. Suddenly shy, she said, "I actually came because I have good news. I got into Harvard. Early decision acceptance. I got the phone call a few days ago, but since I knew I'd be in town this weekend, I wanted to tell you in person."

"And you didn't think to tell me that the second you came in?"

"You seemed distracted."

I hugged her hard, so proud that I was bursting at the seams.

"If the old man decides not to give you your inheritance because of me," I said solemnly, "I'll do whatever I can to make sure you go to Harvard. I swear it."

"Student loans are a thing, in case you didn't know."

"You're not going into debt that'll follow you the rest of your life. And especially at an Ivy League." I leaned back against the couch cushions. "Why couldn't you have gone to school in the UK or Ireland again? Where you don't have to pay out the arse for a college education?"

"Because I didn't want to."

I snorted. "Of course that'd be your answer."

"I wanted to celebrate my acceptance with you and Mari." Niamh fiddled with her hair. "She was nice."

I didn't say anything, because what could I say to that?

"So you're just going to let her go? Even though you love her?" said Niamh.

"It's better this way. I'm not meant for marriage. Romance. All of that. It's bullshite."

Niamh squinted at me. "So wait—are you saying you don't love me?"

"You're my sister. It's different."

"Okaaaaay. That makes no sense, but whatever. Why do you think you're not meant for marriage? And don't you love Mari? So I'm confused."

I groaned. I didn't need my little sister playing armchair shrink tonight. It didn't help that I was as confused as she was.

"Because in case you you've already forgotten, I fucked all this up. And Mari doesn't want me. It's better to let things end than force the issue. Besides, Da showed me that the men in this family aren't loyal. Who's to say I won't do to Mari what he did to Mam?"

"Wow, here I thought you couldn't get any dumber, but you've proven me wrong." Niamh widened her eyes comically. "Mari clearly loves you. I saw it when I was here. She had goo-goo eyes and everything. It was disgusting. I could barely eat around you two."

"That was lust, not love."

"Ew, gross. I do not need to know about your sex life." Niamh gagged. "And believe me, I'm around girls giving guys goo-goo eyes all the time. Mari had it bad. And why would she agree to some stupid deal with you if she didn't kinda sorta care?"

Hope bloomed inside me, but I quashed it ruthlessly. "No, you're wrong."

"Excuse you, I am always right."

"You're seventeen. That's not possible."

"Okay, fine. But I'm just saying: don't let Mari go just because our own parents were messed up. Da left because he made that choice. You'll make your own choice. Duh, Liam."

I reached over and gave my sister a noogie, which she protested so loudly I was sure the neighbors would call the cops.

"Liam, leave me alone!"

"I had to make things normal again. Now I'm the older brother who's so wise and you're the silly little sister."

"You didn't have to mess up my hair for that!"

Niamh glared at me, which made me laugh for the first time in ages.

My thoughts drifted, and I didn't realize Niamh had picked up the photos of Mari I'd left on the coffee table before it was too late.

Her mouth formed a little O of surprise.

"Oh my," she breathed. Her cheeks turned red. "Oh, wow. Um, I shouldn't be looking at these." She tossed them away like they were on fire. "But, um, if you think Mari isn't in love with you—you're wrong. Totally wrong. Even I, a dumb teenager, can see that."

I picked up the photos, my heart lurching inside my chest. I stared down at the photo of Mari kissing the back of my hand, and I knew I couldn't let her go. Not without a fight.

CHAPTER TWENTY-THREE

MARI

The following Monday, I went into work, entered Leslie's office after a single knock, and handed her my letter of resignation.

Too bad she didn't even look up when I entered. She was just typing away on her computer. She waved a hand at me.

"Sit down. I'll be with you in a second."

I sat down. Five minutes passed in silence, Leslie ignoring me entirely. Two more minutes passed.

Finally, I stood up and set the letter on her keyboard, forcing her to recognize my existence.

"What is this?"

"I'm quitting," I said.

Leslie picked up the letter, dangling it from her fingers like I'd handed her a dead bird.

"Excuse me?"

"I'm quitting."

Sighing, Leslie set the letter down, not even bothering to open it. She steepled her fingers and gestured for me to sit down.

I didn't sit again.

After the conversations with my sisters and my mom, I'd realized that Liam had been right: I'd been playing it safe my entire life. I'd thought I could avoid a broken heart that way. I thought if I just did what was wise, secure, *normal*, I'd never have to be afraid that a person I loved would leave me.

But I couldn't live my life in the shadows anymore.

So, first things first: quit my shitty job and pursue my dream of becoming a makeup artist. Finally becoming the person I'd always wanted to be.

"I've decided to enroll in cosmetology school," I said.

"Cosmetology school? At your age?" Leslie looked at me like I'd told her I wanted to become a ballet dancer at sixty-five. "Are you sure about that?"

"Totally sure."

"You realize you'll have to work for yourself. You'll have terrible benefits, if any. Much lower pay than what you get here." She leaned toward me, her expression serious. "What can I do to make you stay?"

Six months ago, Leslie could've convinced me that I should stay. A twenty-cent raise and I would've returned to my desk like the good little employee I was.

"Thank you, but I've made up my mind."

Leslie's lip curled, but then she shrugged. "It's your life. Just don't say I didn't warn you. You understand, right?" She returned to her computer, and I knew I was officially dismissed.

When I arrived back at Dani and Jacob's later that afternoon, the condo was deserted. Not wanting to be alone—Dani's cat Kevin wasn't exactly the greatest company—I walked to Buds and Blossoms, where I found Dani with a customer.

I hadn't been to our family's shop in a few months. Not since things with David had exploded in my face. Back then, both Dani and I were having our share of love problems. Now I was the one with a husband who'd disappeared, while Dani was happily engaged to Jacob.

"Oh, Mari, I'm glad you're here," said Dani after the customer left.

"Do you need me to trim some stems in the back?"

"Well, yeah, but also—" Dani pulled out a card that she'd stowed under the counter. "This was addressed to the store, but it's for you."

"For me?" The card had no return address. Frowning, I opened it, wondering if it was just junk mail that had been forwarded to the wrong address. Until I read what was inside.

Liam Gallagher
Photography show
February 21
The Eye Art Gallery
Belltown, Seattle

And to confirm that this was from Liam himself, a scrawled note in the corner, *please come, a ghrá geal. I miss you.*

"What is it?" Dani took the card from my limp fingers. "Oh. Wow. Oh my God."

I needed to lie down. I needed smelling salts. Or maybe a stiff drink.

So I decided on the next best thing: sitting on the floor, hugging my knees to my chest.

Dani crouched down beside me, saying my name. I felt like I was floating. I felt like—I was totally confused.

"He could've just texted me," I croaked.

Dani pursed her lips. "Men are so fucking dramatic. Why women are the ones called drama llamas, I don't know. Yesterday, Jacob got upset when I bought the wrong kind of coffee for the French press. He acted like it was an affront to humanity."

I took in a deep breath. And then another. My scalp prickled. It was like my body had been numb this entire time but was finally returning to life.

"He misses me," I whispered, staring at those six words in his distinctive handwriting.

"What does this mean?" Dani pointed to the Gaelic words. "I hope it's a compliment."

It must be that nickname he'd said meant "wife." But for whatever reason, I didn't believe it. He hadn't looked me in the eye when he'd said it.

Before that night, I'd tried Googling it multiple times, but I'd had no idea how to spell it. Google kept thinking I'd meant to search for agar gel, like I was in desperate need of a vegan option for gelatin in these trying times.

I typed the words into my phone. When the result pulled up, I couldn't breathe.

My bright one. When had he started calling me that? It felt like ages ago.

I showed Dani the result. She let out a breath and then sat down beside me.

"So, what was the issue?" she said. "That you didn't love him? Or you didn't believe that he loved you?"

"Both. Neither. I don't know." I sighed, rubbing my temples. "He's everything I thought I didn't want in a man. He's not…safe."

"Love isn't safe, but that's what makes it fun."

I leaned my head on my sister's shoulder, and she patted my cheek.

"So I guess I should go to this photography show," I said.

"If you don't, I'll kill you for being the stupidest thing on this planet. And that's saying something because Kevin tried to eat a plastic bag today. So you'd be even dumber than my cat."

I snorted. "Glad I can always count on you for support."

THE NIGHT of Liam's show, I was so nervous that I couldn't eat all day. My hands shook as I put on my makeup. My hair had to be put up in a bun because I couldn't manage to hold the curling iron without burning my ears. By the time I arrived at the gallery, I was a frazzled, sweaty mess, despite the fact that it was all of forty degrees outside and bound to rain tonight.

I was determined to apologize, at the very least. Most of all, to tell Liam I loved him. Even if he no longer loved me, at least I would be honest finally.

Entering the gallery, I looked for Liam, only to see lots of people who were not Liam. The crowd was large enough that I bumped people's shoulders as I wound my way through the gallery. I snagged a glass of white wine to brace myself.

It was only when I was near the back of the gallery, the lights dimmer here, that I actually *looked* at the photos. The one in front of me was at least six by six feet, so huge that it took up the entire wall on which it hung.

But what made my heart stop in my chest wasn't the photo's size: it was the subject.

It was *me.*

It was one of the photos Liam had taken that last night we'd had together. I didn't have makeup on; my hair was messy. Memories flooded me: Liam unbuttoning my wedding gown. Liam kissing me. Liam telling me he wanted to make this marriage real.

And staring at this photo, I saw in that woman's eyes that she adored the man taking her photo. Anyone could see it. And it was so beautiful yet so painful at the same time that I struggled to breathe.

"You came," said a voice that had haunted my dreams for weeks now.

I couldn't move, though. I was pretty certain I'd collapse onto the floor into a heap.

"You sent me an invitation," I said quietly as Liam joined me.

"Didn't mean you'd really come."

I swallowed the last bit of my wine, feeling instantly woozy. Or maybe it was from seeing Liam for the first time in weeks. He looked the same, of course. Just as devastatingly handsome as I'd remembered him. But he seemed a little thinner, his eyes not as bright as I'd remembered. He looked…wary.

"I'm sorry," I blurted. "I'm so, so, sorry." I tried to take Liam's arm, but I missed. Whoa, what was up with that?

"How much wine have you had?" he grumbled, taking my glass and handing it to a server.

"Only that one glass."

"Seems you getting drunk and making poor decisions is going to become a theme with us."

"Hey! I am not drunk!" My words were belied by me grabbing onto Liam's shirt when the gallery started spinning.

To my immense embarrassment, Liam picked me up and carried me into a backroom. People whispered and pointed at us, and I buried my face in his shoulder.

"That was so dramatic," I mumbled. He sat me down on a ratty, blue chair that had definitely seen better days. "You couldn't have just taken my arm?"

"You were going to faint."

"I was not."

His lips curled into a smile as he crouched in front of me. "Still love to argue as much as ever."

I wrinkled my nose. "Only with you. I'm very nice to other people."

"That's because you don't let them see the real you."

I cupped his cheek, reveling in the scratchy feeling of his beard against my palm.

"I looked up what *a ghrá geal* means. Why didn't you tell me the truth?"

"Did you now? And what did you think?"

"That I love you so much the thought of never seeing you again broke my heart."

His eyes widened. "Mari."

"If you don't feel the same—I won't blame you." I fiddled with my purse. "You were right. I was afraid, and I made a huge mistake."

"Mari, look at me."

I did. Because I had to be brave now.

"I love you. I love you so much I'm dying with it. I'm sorry for what I said. It was uncalled for."

"No, it wasn't. I mean, maybe some of it. But most of it was just brutally honest."

"It doesn't matter. Just tell me you love me again."

I smiled. "I love you."

He growled and hauled me into his lap, kissing me so hard that I was afraid I really would faint. He tasted like whiskey. He tasted like my husband.

I smiled. "How do you say it in Gaelic? Let's try that one on for size."

"*Mo ghrá thu.*"

I repeated the words, mangling them terribly. He laughed.

"I love you," he said in English. "So much. I'm sorry for what I said to you that day at the park. I was an arse. A gobshite. A pox."

"You Irish have the best insults."

He kissed me again, his tongue sliding into my mouth. I kissed him back just as fiercely. If there weren't a hundred people right outside this unlocked door, I'd rip his clothes off right here.

After a kiss that seemed to last forever, he said, "I want to make this marriage a real one. I want to marry you—for real this time. The ceremony, the dress, the ridiculous amount of money spent on stupid shite. Like what are those things called? Boutonnières?"

I giggled. "We'll have all the boutonnières. Every single person will wear one. Even my sister's cat. It helps that my family kind of specializes in the whole flower thing, so it won't cost us a dime."

Liam's expression turned serious at the mention of money. "I told Niamh everything."

"And?"

"And she thinks I'm an idiot."

"We're both idiots."

Liam sighed, kissing the side of my neck. "I'm waiting for the ax to fall. The old man hasn't contacted me—yet."

"But if we're staying married, does it matter? And besides, if your grandfather decides to be a jerk, we'll figure out a way to get your sister to the college she wants to go to."

Liam looked shy all of a sudden, which wasn't something I'd ever seen him be. "I don't want you to think I want to make this marriage real only for my sister. I want you in my life. I want you to be my wife: not just for six months, but for always."

I leaned my forehead against his. "Good, because I want the same thing. And even if you didn't, I'd haunt you until you changed your mind."

"My vicious *leanan sídhe*," he said affectionately. Then he smiled, a proud smile that made my heart sing. "Niamh got into Harvard. She just found out."

I hugged him hard, and then we fell onto the floor in a heap of laughter and kisses. Suddenly that unlocked door didn't matter. Not when Liam was pushing my dress up my thighs and pulling my tights down at the same time—

Right then, the door opened. A woman gasped, while another woman said, "Oh my! I didn't know there was going to be a show like this, too."

"Karen, don't be ridiculous," the gasping woman said. "This isn't a peep show."

"Could've fooled me."

I realized my underwear was showing. Liam swore and got up to hustle the women out the door.

"*A ghrá gel*, what are you laughing for?" he said, helping me to stand up.

The giggles kept coming. "Did you see their faces? I think we scarred them for life."

"Let them bitch and moan. Because I've locked the door and am going to finally enjoy my wife again."

And Liam being Liam, he always kept his promises.

I married my wife a year and a half after I married her the first time.

I'd wanted to do it much sooner, until I'd realized that Mari had planned to use the wedding things she'd bought for her wedding with David for our wedding.

"I already have almost everything we need," she'd said, rather too calmly for my liking. "I'd rather use all of it if I could."

To that, I'd countered that there was no way in hell that I was allowing anything that had to do with her weasel of an ex at our wedding. Mari had thought I was being ridiculous, so I'd seduced her until she'd finally agreed with me.

So, the idea for a summer wedding that first year went out the window. A year would put us in the wintertime, which Mari refused to plan a wedding for.

So, it had taken eighteen bloody months to plan, primarily because Mari had got the idea to have the wedding in Ireland. Which sounded great, until you considered how much of a pain it was to work with wedding people on the other side of the world. Mari had almost lost her mind trying to get her wedding planner to respond to her emails as quickly as she expected her to.

Americans have no bloody patience, I tell you. Then again, I was an Irishman impatient to marry my wife a second time. I'd like for the record to show that she'd been the one taking her time, not me.

Mari had also been occupied starting her business as a makeup artist, including creating YouTube videos for her brand-new channel. She'd already been approached by a major brand and was gaining followers and clients faster than she'd ever expected. I wasn't surprised, though: my wife was fucking amazing. And it also meant that I had a talented makeup artist to recommend to my photography clients. Win-win situation.

"You ready?" said Sam as I put on my tuxedo coat. "I was so nervous at my wedding I almost threw up on my shoes."

"I remember. I'm already married to her, you know. So there's no need to be nervous."

"Doesn't matter. Weddings are fucking terrifying. Even when you're not the one saying 'I do.'"

I looked at myself in the mirror, wearing a tuxedo for my own wedding. I had believed for so long that I'd never marry that it was almost surreal to think I was doing it. Twice over. Anticipation jangled inside me.

I wanted to make Mari mine in front of our friends and families. I'd married her once for myself already. This time, I'd marry her to show everyone else I was completely, absolutely in love with her.

The ceremony was outside, the green hills of Ireland making a stunning backdrop. But I didn't care if a fucking leprechaun ran down the aisle: I wanted to see Mari in that white wedding dress, coming toward me and pledging herself to me.

The sounds of the cellist and violinist signaled the start of the ceremony. Our wedding party—Mari's two sisters, Jacob, Niamh, Sam, and my cousin Lochlann Gallagher, a mechanical engineering professor at University of Ireland, Dublin, and who I'd reconnected with in the last year—walked down the grassy aisle with wide smiles on their faces.

And missing from the wedding? Old man Gallagher. It wasn't that we wouldn't have invited him. No, he'd had a heart attack and kicked the bucket two weeks after Mari and I got back together.

Because my life was really that fucking ironic. Sometimes I was sure he'd croaked knowing about me and Mari, but he'd enjoyed the thought of my suffering right before he'd taken his last breath. But he hadn't disinherited Niamh after all.

I couldn't regret any of what had happened in the last eighteen months. Because it had brought me the extraordinary woman now walking toward me with love shining from her eyes.

What a lucky bastard I was.

When Mari reached me, her arm through her father's, I nodded at Mr. Wright. He nodded back. He'd come around recently to my marriage with his oldest daughter. It had helped that I'd introduced him—through Lochlann—to one of the most exclusive growers of orchids in Ireland.

"Take care of her," said Mr. Wright as he wiped away a stray tear. He kissed Mari's cheek. "You look beautiful, sweetheart."

"Thanks, Dad."

I took my wife's hand, looking at her from head to toe. She'd bought a new wedding dress for our wedding, and although she'd looked beautiful in the one I'd pretty much torn off of her eighteen months ago, she looked even more beautiful in this new one.

She also wore the engagement ring I'd bought her the day after we'd made up. Rose gold, morganite, with the words *A ghrá geal* engraved on it.

Mari's dress this time was simple, white, silky. Something probably way more complicated to it than I'd ever understand, but I was already imagining taking it off my wife tonight.

"You look amazing," I mouthed as the officiant began speaking.

Mari dimpled. "So do you."

Yeah, that dress didn't stand a chance tonight. I just hoped she didn't spend too much on it because it was going to end up in shreds.

When we were finally pronounced husband and wife, I yanked my wife into my arms, dipped her over my arm, and kissed her until I heard my sister say, "Get a room, you two."

Now, hours later, I was slow-dancing with my wife at our reception. I had one more song in me before I was taking her away to our hotel and having her all to myself.

Mari, though, seemed distracted. She kept looking over my shoulder.

"What is it?" I said.

She looked sheepish. "Nothing."

"Tell me, wife."

"It's Kate. She's disappeared."

"Fairies probably took her away. Can't say I'm upset about

it. She's a pain."

Mari pinched me, which just made me kiss her until she was breathless.

"No, really," she said, "I'm worried. She tends to not think before she acts."

"Your sister is an adult. She can manage on her own."

"That's what worries me," muttered Mari.

Now twenty-one, Kate was almost a bigger pain in the arse than my own sister. At least Niamh was too busy with attending Harvard to get into trouble—as far as I knew. Kate, though, seemed destined for trouble no matter what. It didn't help that she was as smart as my own sister. If those two ever teamed up, they'd take over the world, I thought with a shudder.

"Look, there she is," I said. Kate had just sat down at a nearby table, looking rather rumpled. "She must've gone off with one of the guests."

"Kate doesn't date. She thinks men are idiots." Mari lifted her eyebrows. "Her words, not mine."

"What, is she gay?"

"Noooooo. At least I don't think so. She's just…particular."

To my surprise, my cousin Lochlann soon sat down at a table across from Kate, looking similarly rumpled. Lochlann was in his thirties, and according to women, ridiculously handsome. In my mind, he was the intense professor who'd been obsessed with building things when we were kids.

I was tempted to tell Mari about Lochlann's rumpled appearance, but she'd only get "into a dither," as she liked to say sometimes. And I wasn't about to let my wife get distracted from me tonight.

"Let's get out of here." I palmed her arse. "I'm dying for you, *a ghrá geal*."

She cupped my cheek. "Same. But first I have to tell you something. I was going to save it for later, but…"

"You're wearing that butt plug from Vegas."

She pursed her lips. "I'm not that much of a masochist. Wearing it all day? Ugh, no."

"Don't worry. I brought it with me to use tonight."

Her eyes sparkled, but she didn't tell me no. *Excellent.*

But soon my mind was on other things when she looked up and said, "I'm pregnant."

"What?" My voice was strained. "How?"

"Well, when a man and a woman love each other very much—"

My heart soared. I was so happy I was about to burst.

"Are you serious? You aren't messing with me?"

"Took the test two days ago. You knocked me up." She touched my cheek. "Even when I'm on the pill, too. So good job, there."

I puffed out my chest, absurdly proud. "Irish sperm. Premium make."

"You're an idiot, but I love you." Her voice softened as she asked, "Are you happy, then?"

All seriousness now, I said, "I thought the happiest day of my life was me marrying you the first time."

I cupped my wife's cheek. "But I was wrong—because it's today, the day you married me a second time and told me I was gonna be a da."

And then I swooped down and carted her off to our room to celebrate the best way I knew how—butt plugs and all.

ABOUT THE AUTHOR

A coffee addict and cat lover, Iris Morland writes sexy and funny contemporary romances. If she's not reading or writing, she enjoys binging on Netflix shows and cooking something delicious.

www.ingramcontent.com/pod-product-compliance
Lightning Source LLC
Chambersburg PA
CBHW050346190726
48284CB00007BB/2170